CONTROL IS JACK

CONTROL IS JACK

JOHN ANDES

iUniverse LLC
Bloomington

Control is Jack

iUniverse books may be ordered through booksellers or by contacting:

iUniverse LLC
1663 Liberty Drive
Bloomington, IN 47403
www.iuniverse.com
1-800-Authors (1-800-288-4677)

ISBN: 978-1-4917-0563-6 (sc)
ISBN: 978-1-4917-0564-3 (ebk)

Printed in the United States of America

iUniverse rev. date: 08/26/2013

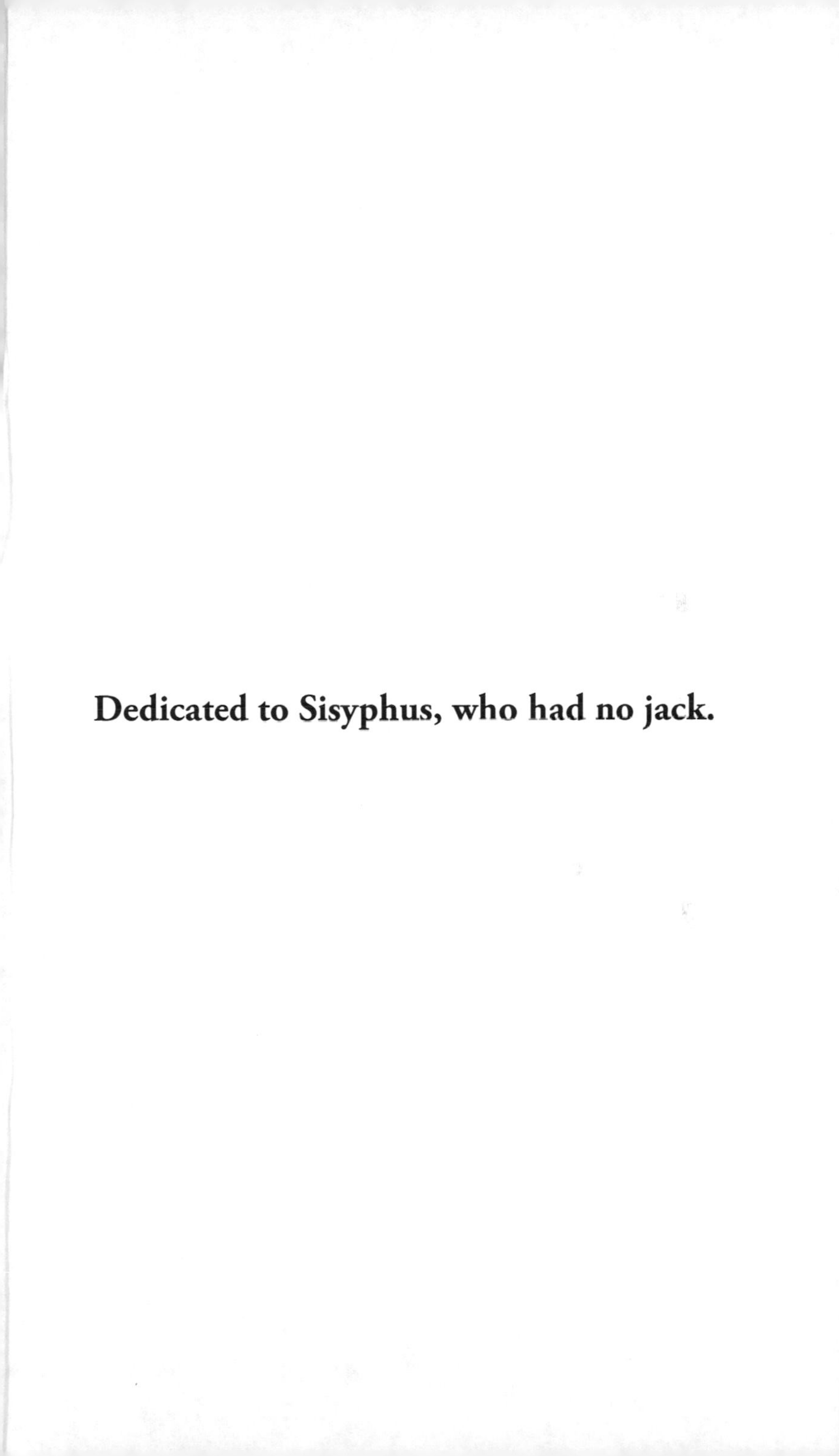

Dedicated to Sisyphus, who had no jack.

I

"Thank you for calling Sun Shine Travel, this is Travel Coordinator Denton. How may I help you?"

"I was calling to see about this vacation I won."

"Sir, look on the certificate. Do you have the certificate in front of you? On the certificate at the upper left-hand corner, you'll see a certificate number. It starts with two letters and has five numbers. Do you see it? Will you read it to me?"

"If I give you the certificate number, I ain't bought nothin' have I?"

"No, sir. I need the number to activate your award and to verify that we sent the proper certificate to the correct individual."

"OK. The number is AJ57493."

"Thank you, sir. Now if you can hold for a moment, I have to go to the main frame and enter your certificate number. This will lock it out. That means no one else will have access to or can take your award. Can you hold?"

"Sure, but I ain't buyin' nothin'."

"Sir, I just want to make sure you have all the details of the award and that no one else can access your award before you get all the details. Then you can decide if you want the award. OK? I'll be back in a moment. Thanks for holding."

Time to take a pee and get a cup of coffee while the fish circles the bait. The on-hold message will soften him up. Testimonials from happy vacationers. Phony background sounds of surf, island music, and children. Voices are those of the telemarketers. Paid $50 each.

"Thanks for holding. Sorry it took so long, but there were a few other people waiting to claim your award. I had to verify the exact time of your call. You beat them out by six seconds. It's officially your award. Now, how can I help you?"

"I need to know the details of these vacations."

"That makes sense. The certificate can only give you a brief outline of the award. It's only a sheet of paper, right?"

"Yah, right."

"Before I start, let me remind you that you called on our special 800 telephone number. And, therefore, this call is not costing you a penny. Second, I want to give you all the details of the award. So, please feel free to ask any question anytime during my explanation of the details. Don't be bashful. Interrupt if there is something I am not making clear to you. OK?"

"OK."

"First, a few details. Let me verify your name and address. Are you Matthew T. Johns?"

"Yes."

"And, Mr. Johns, do you reside at 3414 London Road in Green Bay, Wisconsin, Zip Code 78656."

"Yes, all that's correct."

"Great. I would like to suggest, if you haven't done so already, make sure you have a pen and a pad of paper in front of you to take down any notes on the details I'm about to give you. OK."

"Way ahead of you."

"Great."

The fish's mouth is open.

"Your award consists of three separate vacations, which can be taken individually or all at one time. And, you have three years to take the vacations. It's sort of like a vacation bank account. You can withdraw parts of your award or take the whole award whenever you want. I say whenever you want, because there are no blackout times during the year.

I'm sure you've heard of blackout times. Those are the times during the year when the resorts, motels, and hotels are booked solid, because these are prime vacation times. The blackout times for all other vacation trips, but not these, are the last two weeks in November, mid-December to mid—January, and the week before Easter. But, you don't have to worry about blackout times. That's the beauty of your award.

You can take the vacations whenever you want. You can take the vacations when the snow is piled up to your front door and the wind chill factor is – 30. You can escape for fun in the sun and come back all tanned and relaxed ready to face the winter. You can take your vacations, while your friends can't even get reservations. All we ask is that you make your reservation 90 days in advance of your arrival at one of the vacation resorts. You'll be able to do that, right? 90 days is OK with you, right?"

"Yah, 90 days in advance is no problem. Emma can't get off work too easy. I can, 'cause I'm a general contractor. I'm my own boss. Emma is a nurse at St. Luke's hospital. She has a lot of people she has to answer to. So, 90 days is fine."

"That's great. You and your wife and up to two children are entitled to take these vacations. The children can stay in the room with you and your wife. Do you have young children, who you would like to take along with you, Mr. Johns?"

"Our kids are grown. Matt Jr. is married and lives in Minneapolis. He's got two kids. Sarah works in sales in Milwaukee. Not married yet. So we won't be takin' the kids with us. They're too old. Besides that, it's not their free vacation prize, it's mine."

"Great. You and your wife are entitled to five days and four nights in Orlando, the home of Disney World. Have you ever been to Disney World, sir?"

"No."

"Well, you'll love it. It's the only place in the world where you are supposed to act like a kid. Play. Go for rides. Swim in the pool. Sleep late. Eat too much junk food. You know, just like a kid. While you're visiting Disney, you'll be staying at the luxurious Emperada Resort. Generous suites. Each one-bedroom suite has a living room and its own kitchenette. So you can be more comfortable than in an ordinary motel room. There are three swimming pools, tennis courts, and a golf course for guests at the Emperada Resort. Do you play golf or tennis, sir?"

"No, never had the time to learn."

"Well, there are teaching pros at the Resort. And you can rent clubs or a tennis racquet if you'd like to get some exercise. There is also a three-mile parcour for jogging and fitness, if you like that type of exercise. Given the carefree environment, you certainly won't have to work off any stress."

"Is the resort actually on the Disney Property?"

"No sir, it's not. And that's the beauty of the resort. No noisy crowds to ruin your time. The resort is five miles from Disney World. There are free trams every half-hour to and from Disney World. So, it's real easy for you and your wife to get to the theme park, have a great time, and then get back to the resort whenever you want. You have the best of both worlds . . . the rides and excitement of Disney and the relaxation of the resort. And the transportation to and from Disney is free and frequent. Does that sound like a great time?"

"Sounds good."

"While you're a guest at the Emperada Resort, you are entitled to a complimentary continental breakfast every morning."

"What about lunch and dinner?"

"Those meals are your choice. We would not want to hamper your vacation by requiring you to eat at a specific restaurant at a predetermined time. We want you to be free to take advantage of the many and diverse meal offerings, both at the resort and the restaurants nearby. If you like French, Chinese, Japanese, Italian, or just good old fashioned American prime beef, it's all available to you at your convenience.

I say convenience, because, while you are in Florida, you will have a rental car at your disposal. The daily rental, up to five days and the mileage are free. You will be responsible for insurance, sales tax, and any gasoline you use. But, the rental and mileage are free. In the evening, you and your wife can take a short drive to any of the seven three-star restaurants in the neighborhood. The car will be waiting for you at the airport when you arrive in Florida."

"I can use the car to go anywhere?"

"Anywhere in the state of Florida, sir. You could go to Lake Okachobee or over to the East Coast beaches for the day. But, the contract with the rental company prohibits using the car to travel outside the state. And, because you will be driving a rental car, I am legally required to ask you three questions. Are you over the age of 21? Do you have a valid driver's license? And, do you carry in-force automobile insurance?"

"I'm way past 21. Both Emma and I have valid driver's licenses. Our car insurance is paid for the year."

They pay in advance. They have money.

"Thank you, sir. Those are just some minor, but very important details I have to confirm before we go on."

"You can set your air transportation to and from each of your vacations. That's a real plus. You're not locked into someone else's preset schedule. You have the flexibility to tailor your vacations to best suit your personal schedule. These are not pre-planned tours. These are your vacations. Your second vacation. Actually, it is second on my computer screen. And I think on the certificate in front of you. This vacation can be taken first, second or third. It's your choice, because these are your vacations. That's one of the beauties of this award. You have the freedom to go where ever you want whenever you want any time of the year during the three years."

"The second vacation is three nights and four days on Grand Bahamas Island. Have you ever been to a Caribbean island, Sir?"

"Never."

"You and your wife will love the long sunny days and the comfortable breezy nights. To get to the Bahamas, you'll take a day cruise on the Big Red Boat. Have you ever taken a cruise, Sir?

"Never."

"Well, you're in for a special treat. The ship leaves Fort Lauderdale before mid morning and you and your wife will spend six hours lounging on the deck, soaking up the sun, listening to steel bands, and sipping special tropical drinks. Do you like games of chance, Sir?"

"Like what?"

"Like roulette, craps, and black jack."

"Yeah, me and Emma, go up to the lodge for bingo twice a month and we've been to the Chippewa Palace a few times since it opened. Real exciting. Did OK, too."

"On the Captain's Deck, you'll find a full-sized casino, if you choose to come in from the fresh air and sun. But, promise to go easy at the gaming tables. Don't take them for all their money. OK?"

"OK."

"You will be responsible for the port fees before boarding the ship. These are like the sales tax on the rental car. We can't control or collect the taxes or fees. They must be taken care of by the individual, whose name is on the award. It's the law."

"What are the port fees for and how much are they?"

"The port fees are international taxes paid to the country of the ship's registry. In this case the fees are paid to the government of Liberia. It's the way that government earns revenue from the ship. Fees are levied any time of year. In the peak vacation season they are higher than during the off-season. According to the files for last year, the fees range from $28-$79. I think that is a safe range. Is that OK?"

"Yah, how much is the sales tax in Florida?"

"7%. And that is on everything, but food from the grocery store. OK?"

"Yah, we got a sales tax and an income tax. Every government wants its due."

"When you arrive at the Bahamas, your accommodations will be at the Silver Sands Resort. This is a comfortable, family resort nestled on the leeward side of the island ten minutes from the hustle and bustle of down town. The Silver Sands has its own private beach and tennis courts. So, you can just relax on the shore and fall asleep listening to the gentle waves. Whenever you want, you and your wife can take a leisurely stroll to the center of town.

Shop the duty free stores. That's where you could really use your winnings from the casino on the Big Red Boat. Luxury items . . . jewelry, perfume, china, silverware, designer clothing . . . nearly 75% below retail prices. There is no taxation or duty paid to bring the items with you back to Green Bay. You can buy unique gifts for your family and friends for a fraction of the U.S. retail price. You and your wife will look like big spenders without spending big. Does your wife like to shop?"

"In the shopping department, she's the queen. She can spend all day and all her pay at the mall on a given Saturday."

"Well, maybe you better steer her away from the shops on the Grand Bahamas. Or, at least limit what she can spend. Give her an allowance. I remember my wife and took this vacation. Janet went down town from the Silver Sands and went ballistic at the stores. Fortunately, her credit card has a limit. Or else, I think she would have bought everything in sight."

"Yah, I'll have to watch Emma. She loves to spoil the children and grand kids. Did you go on this vacation?"

"Yes, sir. It's company policy. All of the service representatives go through a rigorous training program. We take the vacation trips, stay at the resorts, travel on the Big Red Boat, and eat at the restaurants. When we return, we are required to file a very detailed report covering all the facets of our trip. We can even offer suggestions for improvement. This way when we talk to an award winner like you, we can honestly answer any questions raised during our conversation. We've been on a kind of test-drive. What we find to be good enough is considered too good enough for others. If we don't like the vacations, Sun Shine will fix the problem. Does that make sense?"

"Yah."

"After your stay on the Bahamas, you and your wife will return to the ship for a romantic moonlight cruise back to Fort Lauderdale."

"I have a question. When we are on the island, do we get a rental car?"

"No, sir. A car is not necessary for your stay on this lovely Caribbean Island. Everything you would want to see or do is within a ten to fifteen minute walk. If you would like to tour the island, the Desk Clerk at the Silver Sands can recommend the appropriate tour bus."

"What do we do when we arrive in the states?"

"You are free to do as you wish. And here is where I can give you some personal advice. My suggestion is to take the Bahamas vacation first and the Disney vacation second. That way, your rental car is waiting for you when you return from your cruise in Fort Lauderdale. You can then drive to Orlando and sleep at the Emperada. The drive is less than three hours. Also, this way you only have to book one airfare and not two. You can fly into Fort Lauderdale, take the cruise, relax at the Silver Sands, return on the Big Red Boat, stay at the Emperada, and fly back to Green Bay from Orlando. One long fun-filled, sun-filled, relaxing roundtrip. But, that is only a suggestion. You are free to take the vacations in any order and at anytime you wish. Does that make sense to you, sir? Can you take a nine-day vacation?"

"Sure, in the winter, contracting is slow. Mostly simple repair work. And Emma has a ton of time she is due. Nine days would be no big deal."

"Great. I can see you both now returning to Green Bay as brown as walnuts. Your arms loaded with duty-free gifts for your children and grandchildren."

"You third vacation is four nights and five days in Cancun Mexico. Sir, have you ever been to Mexico?"

"No."

"Well, you are in for a special treat. The food, the weather, the scenery, and the energy. Here is one place you and your wife can really enjoy yourself as adults. The people of Cancun seem to go round the clock. And if you're looking for a place to blow off a little steam, this is it. Maybe you or your wife has had a particularly stress-filled time. Then Cancun is the ideal place for you. While in Cancun, you'll stay at the Posada Laguna. This is a medium-sized super friendly resort. Not one of the impersonal monsters further down on the beach.

I'm sure you've seen pictures of the huge hotels on the beach at Cancun. Forty stories high. Eighty rooms to a floor. The places are fashioned after the monster hotels of Las Vegas. Not very friendly. People who stay there are not guests, just numbers. You know, room 3842 or room 2765. But, the Posada Laguna is different. The Posada Laguna is dedicated to individual service of the highest order. Personal service for each of their special guests. Just like the finest European hotels. And, here is the beauty of staying at the Posada Laguna. You can walk to the pleasure palaces, enjoy the dancing, the music, whatever, and return to the relaxation and sanity of your own resort. I also suggest you take a one-day tour of the Mayan ruins. Nothing like it. History and beauty in one. Does that sound good to you, Sir?"

"Yah."

"I have a special hint for this vacation. If you hail a cab and one arrives with its windows down, don't take it. Windows down means no air conditioning. Windows up means air conditioning. You're on vacation in Mexico. You deserve air conditioning. Now, let me summarize. You get three separate vacations, which you and your wife can take in any sequence, in any combination at any time over the next three years. There are no blackout periods. You can take these vacations . . . Disney World, Grand Bahamas, and Cancun, Mexico when you want. Do you have any questions?"

"Yes just a few. How do we get to these vacations?"

"You are free to book air travel anyway you wish. Through your local travel agent or you can use Sun Shine Travel Flight Services. We are one of the nation's ten largest bookers of airline travel. Because of the volume of business we have with all national carriers, the rates they offer us are the lowest available. And we pass these savings along to our clients, because we want them to be clients for a long time. But, you may want to shop around. Check with an agent in Green Bay, or Chicago. Then check with Sun Shine. You'll see the money we can save. But it's your choice, because these are your vacations."

"Roughly how much would the airfare be to Fort Lauderdale or Orlando?"

"Sir, I have no way of knowing for three reasons. I have no computer access to the airlines price schedule. Two, I don't know when during the year you and your wife will be taking the vacations. And, I don't know when during the next three years you and your wife will take the vacations. However, I do know that when you are ready to take your vacations, Sun Shine Travel Fight Services can offer you the lowest available fare."

"What costs will be my responsibility when we are on vacations?"

"Meals, other than the breakfasts at the Emperada, gasoline and insurance for the rental car, hotel taxes and sales taxes on your purchases, port fees, and general spending money for your enjoyment. The rooms for ten nights, the rental car in the state of Florida, and the cruise to and from the Bahamas are all parts of your award.

Now, we at Sun Shine Travel would like to send you your complete vacation package. This package includes four-color brochures for each destination and resort, a video highlighting your trips, your pre-authorized travel vouchers to be completed by you when you make your reservations, valuable coupons for use at each resort . . . $300 worth of savings for excursions, meals and shopping, and your Sun Shine Travel ID card. We'd like to send your vacation package to Matthew Johns on London Road in Green Bay, Wisconsin.

When you receive the package you can sit with your wife and plan your vacations to suit your schedules. It takes approximately five working days for your vacation package to arrive by registered mail. We have to send it by registered mail, because it is so valuable. At retail pricing its worth over $2000, but not to an award winner. The award has been activated and is pre-authorized. You are ready to travel whenever you decide. To secure your package so that you and your wife can review all the details requires a fee of $599. This can be applied to your credit card. Sun Shine accepts MasterCard, Visa, American Express, and discover. Which one would you prefer to use?"

"Wait a minute. It says here that the vacations are free. That I won the trips."

"Sir, I'm sorry if there is confusion. But, the certificate you received does say that you are entitled to the award. But, it does not say the vacations are free. Now, will that be Visa or MasterCard to secure the $2000 package of vacations for less than $600?"

"I'm not payin' nothing 'til I talk to my wife."

"That makes very good sense, sir. That's why we want to send you and your wife the complete package. The brochures, the video, the itineraries, pre-approved travel vouchers, and the coupons . . . everything. That way you two can sit in the comfort of your own home and discuss how and when you will take the vacations. You'll have all the material in front of you so that you can make a good decision. Would you like to put the $599 on your Visa card?"

"I would not like to spend the money. And what am I spending the money for anyway?"

"The fee covers the costs involved in assembling and processing the vacations, as well as a nominal percentage of the complete vacation package. When the package containing the pre-approved travel vouchers and coupons is mailed to you, it has an estimated value of $2000 to $2500 considering a total of ten nights at the luxuries resorts and the discount coupons. That's what you'd pay if you purchased these vacations at retail. But, because you won the award, your cost is less that $600. You have been selected to save almost $2000 by taking advantage of this award. So, will that be Visa or MasterCard?"

"Let me get back to you after I talk to my wife. I took real good notes. Then, when she is satisfied, we'll call back."

"I'm sorry, sir. The certificate is clear on callbacks. In the center at the bottom of the face, you'll see the red words, *One Call Per Award Winner*. This has been your one call. That's why we want to send the complete package of material to you. You can review it with your wife and decide when you'll take your vacations. I may have failed to mention that these vacations are transferable. That means once you have secured them with a major credit card you may give any one or all of them as a gift or gifts to your adult children.

You and your wife may want to take one trip and give one each to your children. Maybe the Disney vacation for your son and his family. Your grandchildren would love Disney. Then you and your wife can go to either the Bahamas or Cancun and your daughter to the other destination. These vacations could be wonderful gifts for your children. Which card would you like to use?"

"Before I do anything I gotta know if you are legitimate."

"Sir, Sun Shine Travel is one of the ten largest travel agencies in the U.S. We have been promoting our services with special vacation packages for more than five years. We are members of the International Better Business

Bureau, the Tampa Chamber of Commerce, and we are regulated by the Florida Department of Commerce in Tallahassee. By regulation, the Department of Commerce assures you that we deliver what we promise. If we ran promotions in which people didn't get what we promised, their word of mouth, not to mention lawsuits would have put us out of business a long time ago. And since we have been doing this for five years and since we are in the top ten, we must be legitimate. Plus, our practices can be checked with local, state, and international regulators. Which credit card would you like to use?"

"Do you have any telephone numbers for the Better Business Bureau and the Florida Department of Commerce? I'd like to check your company out before I buy anything."

"That makes good sense, sir. The Better Business Bureau Toll Free number is 1-888-438-7573. The Florida Department of Commerce in Tallahassee, Florida is 1-351-456-7890, and then you'll hit extension 8632. After the next prompt, enter the code for Sun Shine Travel. That code is 5671. A voice will confirm our business practices."

"Thank you. I'll call these numbers and get back to you."

"I'm sorry, sir. Once we hang up, if you have not activated your vacations with a credit card, I will have to return to the main frame and delete your name as an award winner. Then the vacations will become part of our promotional treasure chest and made available to another award winner. However, we encourage you to call these numbers during the work hours tomorrow. You'll see we are everything we said we are and more. Now, which card would you like to use? Visa?"

"Can I send the material back to you once my wife and I have looked at it?"

"Sir, why would you send the material back to us once it has been activated in your name?"

"Well, maybe there is something we don't like about it."

"What's not to like? Three great resorts. The freedom to take the vacations in any sequence and combination you choose. The freedom to take the vacations whenever you choose during the next three years. No blackout periods. A saving of over $2000 over the retail price of these resort stays. The freedom to give any part or all of the vacations to your adult children. Would you like to put this on your American Express card?"

"Why not just send the material to us and if we like it, we'll charge it to our Visa?"

"Sir, I'm sorry. We cannot afford to send nearly $3000 worth of pre-authorized and activated travel vouchers in the mail in the hopes that you will pay us for the pre-authorized trips. If you chose not to pay us, you could still use the vacations or give the transferable vouchers to a friend or neighbor. By sending the itineraries and pre-approved vouchers to you to look at without you paying the promotional fee, we are risking a great deal with a little or no chance of reward. But, if you activate the vouchers and itineraries with you credit card, you are free to do with them what you wish."

"What happens if we pay for the trips, get the package and decide that we really don't want to take the vacations?"

"You can give any or all of them to your children. But, wouldn't it be great to spend some quality time with your wife in a romantic tropical resort? Let me ask you.

When was that last time you and your wife got away for a vacation? Got away to somewhere where you can relax, sleep in, nap on the beach, enjoy great meals, and maybe dance into the night. Get the romance juices flowing? This is your chance to surprise your wife. Give her the vacation she has always wanted. Will you be using your MasterCard?"

"But, what if she is upset that I went and did something this big without first talking it over with her? Then what do I do?"

"If she is really upset that you love her and that you wanted to do something special for her, that you wanted to give her a big treat she so richly deserves, then you can give the vacations to your children. Will that be Visa or MasterCard?"

"What if I want to cancel the amount off my credit card after we have looked at the material?"

"Credit card purchasing is the safest in the world. You use a credit card to protect you. The credit card has a contract with you and not with us. The credit card will work for you. If Sun Shine Travel didn't do what the credit cards demand, if we didn't treat their clients fairly, we could not accept payment from their clients. Sun Shine Travel and our business practices have been reviewed and scrutinized by MasterCard, Visa, American Express, and Discover. They all have found that we are reputable and that we treat their clients fairly and honestly. So you can rest assured that you can use your credit card with complete safety. Would you prefer to use Visa or Master Card?"

"You say that once I have given you my credit card for these vacations, if I don't like them I can cancel them through my credit card. Or, once I've paid for the vacations, if I can't use them for whatever reason, I can give them to anyone I wish. I could give them to my kids."

"Yes, sir, that is correct. They are fully transferable to other adults, once the trips have been secured by you and the promotional fee is paid. Would you like to use your Visa card?"

"Yah. Visa and MasterCard. I want two packages. I want one for Emma and me. The kids can get their own vacations. And, I want one for the business. I want to give year-end bonuses to my two foremen and office manager. The Visa card is my personal card and the MasterCard is in the name of MTJ Contractors. How do we do this?"

The axiom of telemarketing: "Control the questions and you control the details. Control the details and you control the situation. Control the situation and you control the outcome. Always remain calm. Always be in control."

Control is the jack. It's the power that drives. It's the juice that flows. It's the adrenaline. While appearing calm, I am pulsing with excitement. It's tough not express elation, because I just got a double. A rarity, but always the possibility if the axiom is followed. I just made $100. With the two I hit earlier, I just doubled my quota for the night. Goin' into Saturday I have twelve. That's $600. Damn I'm good.

Now the paper work. I hope this guy doesn't kick. His cards better be good, or I'll be crushed. Tell him I have to go to the main frame and lock in his vacations so no one can touch them. Take the forms into the supervisor. He processes the card numbers. Waves to me that they are stone cold. Back on the telephone, I tell Mr. Johns that I will transfer him to processing so that they can confirm the mailing address. Does he want the material sent to his home or office?

A double is more intense than getting laid with a bar chick on Saturday night. Conning is the means to both ends. The elation of the hunt and the post success exhaustion are the same. The depth of the post-success depression, whether it's a sale or a fuck, can be heavy. The good side of a double sale is that afterward I don't have to look at or be nice to the person I just screwed. I can seamlessly move on to the next mark. And, do so in five minutes. Faster than I can be ready in bed. But, the pressure of repeating can be tough. Repeat. Repeat. Repeat. Sell the same half-truths. The same implications. The same non-answers.

Over and over and over again. Go through the entire process. Reciting the kind words as if it were the first time they had ever been said. Little dips into the personality or psyche of the caller or the chick to make the pitch sound like not a pitch. Wrapping up each close with a request for my reward. Never letting the fish off the hook until I'm ready to toss them back. Reel them in and let them swim. Shuck and jive. Cajole. Tease. Lie. Give out phony information that sounds real enough to make them feel comfortable enough to bite . . . and give up my reward. I sometimes wonder if the caller or the chick wants to be screwed, and they just make me think that I am in control.

Mine is a confidence game without the three cards. My voice slithers over the telephone, seeking the warmth of his wallet and the wealth within it. Convincing him he has nothing to risk . . . nothing to lose . . . by letting me charge him for something of substantially less value that he thinks. All so I can make $50, if I am good or lucky. Frankly, I'd rather be the latter, but I am the former.

Some weeks the certificates are mailed to a harvestable school of fish. Harvestable for my cohorts and me means naïve, hungry, and possessing valid credit cards, which can carry $599. When these fish are biting, the fisherman's job is easy. They see the bait, bite, and leap into the boat. These are rich weeks. Two hits a shift is easy. Then there are the weeks of fishing when there are no bites. Or, if I'm lucky to get a bite, the carp is so scrawny and poor that the credit card can't carry the charge. He gets tossed back into the sea of humanity, which is the not-so-precise target for our efforts.

Weeks of bad mailings can kill sales. Instead of two a day, the fisherman considers himself lucky to get one a day or, God forbid, four for entire six-shift week. These are weeks of real depression. Most of the people on the nightshift have other jobs or their spouses work. The foray into the fog-enshrouded sea of telemarketing is supplemental revue to them. To me it is my sole source of income. A limited and erratic weekly income to pay large predetermined monthly expenses. The ends do not meet. Hell, they're not in the same universe. I am like a junky constantly chasing the one big score that will make everything right. It never does.

II

"I find for the husband."

With those five words Divorce Court Judge Tim Stanger lifted a huge financial millstone from my neck. Now I can bob to the surface and gasp some fresh air. He accepted my position that my reported income was not as great as it had been when he levied the crushing burden of alimony and child support two years ago. The amounts, based on some arcane bureaucratic formula, were determined before I was dismissed from my real office job.

Now I am a telehuckster with a greatly reduced grab-ass income and no benefits like life, health or dental insurance. Trying to work my way back to the old standard of living. Cutting corners, ignoring the threatening notices from bill collectors, hiding my car from the repo man, and delaying payments. Living in a room behind a garage in a lower-middle income neighborhood. A far cry from the 2/2 condo in the high rise on the water. Ah, how the mighty have fallen. Divorce does that.

Supported by my most recent IRS filing and three months' worth of official pay stubs, the good judge reduced the support payments by 55% a month. He made his decision retroactive to the date of my filing. Therefore, all of the payments in excess of the reduced amount made during the nine months from filing my motion to the judge's decision were awarded as credit. Finally a rule of law that favored me. Hot shit.

Credit. Not much, but I beat the bitch. Now my outgo is within sight of my reported income. Sort of like the top of the mountain is within sight of the base. Now I have to get out of debt . . . all the credit cards, retail accounts, doctors, and private school debts I was awarded originally by the judge. Awarded because *Ms. Rite* had no visible means of income to pay the debts she helped incurred. Most of her reported income was going to Doctors who over-prescribed medications. And the forged prescriptions for the medications. Substance abuse does that. Judge Stanger lifted the millstone off my neck so that I can fight with the sharks that have been circling my bleeding body.

As we are leaving the courtroom, my Ex confronts me . . . tears in her eyes and saliva in the cracks of her mouth.

"You rotten fuck. You lied and cheated. How can you do this to your son? I'll get you. I'll show the court your two trust funds. I'll strip them clean. You'll go to jail for contempt. I'll take everything you have . . . now and in the future."

The bailiff had to restrain her. Her emotional flailing got my juices pumping. I love confrontation and combat.

They can put me in control. It gets me jacked. Maybe that's why I'm so good a telehuckstering. As the bailiff led her down the hall, she turned back to me. I smiled my best Cheshire cat, held up three fingers, and mouthed the words, '*three trust funds.*' The perception that I have vast amounts of money hidden in three trust funds will drive her to spend endless and fruitless hours searching for the Golden Fleeces.

Back to my room. Change. Mickey D's for lunch. Although my shift starts at 4:00, maybe I can pick up some of the over flow callers in queue. This is a B week. In A-weeks I get a paycheck reflecting all my deals. In B-weeks I get a paycheck for my deals up to the two-per shift quota. Any deals I get over the quota for the week are paid to me gross and in cash. The separate envelope provides a real incentive to push for the caller's card. I think I failed to tell the court about the cash in the B weeks.

* * *

"Yes, Ma'am. It's company policy. All of the service representatives go through an extensive training program. We take the vacation trips, stay at the resorts, and travel on the Big Red Boat, and eat at the restaurants. We are required to learn, first hand, about the vacations. Experience what award winners will experience. This way when we talk to an award winner, we can honestly answer any questions during our conversation. Does that make sense?"

"Well, I guess so."

"After your stay on the Bahamas, you and your husband will return to the ship for a romantic moonlight cruise back to Fort Lauderdale."

"When we are on the island, do we get a rental car?"

"A car is not necessary for your stay. Everything you would want to see or do is within a ten to fifteen minute walk. If you would like to tour the island, the Desk Clerk at the Silver Sands can recommend the appropriate native tour bus."

"What do we do when we arrive in the states?"

"You are free to do as you wish. And here is where I can give you some advice based on my taking the trips. My suggestion is to take the Bahamas vacation first and the Disney vacation second. That way, your rental car is waiting for you in Fort Lauderdale when you return from your cruise. You can then drive to Orlando and sleep at the Emperada. The drive is about two hours on a clearly marked interstate highway. Also this way you can book your airfare once and not twice.

You can fly into Fort Lauderdale, take the cruise, relax at the Silver Sands, return on the Big Red Boat, stay at the Emperada, and fly back to Sioux Falls from Orlando. One fun-filled, sun-filled, relaxing round trip. But, that's only my suggestion based on personal experience. You are free to take the vacations in any order and at anytime you wish. Does that make sense to you, ma'am? Can you take a nine-day vacation?"

"I think so."

"Great. I can see you both now returning to Sioux Falls as brown as walnuts. Your arms loaded with duty-free gifts. Expensive and unique gifts you got for a fraction of what you would have paid at home or in Chicago or Minneapolis."

"You third vacation is four nights and five days in Cancun Mexico. Ma'am, have you ever been to Mexico?"

"No."

"Well, you are in for a special treat. The food, the weather, and scenery. Mexico is a wonderful place. The ancient Mayan ruins. The Jungle. The mountains. Three separate one-half day trips to truly experience this exotic land. Immerse your self in a land that is truly foreign to what you're used to in Sioux Falls. I would suggest that you take lots of film for your camera. While in Cancun, you'll stay at the Posada Laguna. This is a medium-sized resort. Not one of the monsters further down on the beach. I'm sure you've seen pictures of the huge hotels on the beach at Cancun. Forty stories high. One hundred rooms to a floor. The places are fashioned after the monster hotels of Las Vegas. Loaded with the party animals. Not very well suited for relaxation.

Now, here is the beauty of staying at the Posada Laguna. You can walk to the great restaurants for a special dinner at the hotels and return to the peace and quiet of your own resort. You get the best of both worlds. Does that sound good to you, ma'am? The sightseeing, the beaches, the great food."

"It does."

"I have a special hint for this vacation. Again, this is based on personal experience. If you hail a cab and one arrives with its windows down, don't take it. Windows down means no air conditioning. Windows up means air conditioning. You're on vacation. You deserve air conditioning. Now, let me summarize. You get three separate vacations, which you and your husband can take in any sequence, in any combination at any time over the next three years. There are no blackout periods. You can take these vacations . . . Disney World, Grand Bahamas, and Cancun, Mexico when you want. Do you have any questions?"

"Yes just a few. How do we get to these vacations? I mean, can we drive or fly to these resorts."

"Well, it would be impossible to drive to the Bahamas. And, Cancun is about a week's drive from Sioux Falls. You could drive to Disney. Or, you're free to book air travel anyway you wish. Through your local travel agent or you can use Sun Shine Travel Flight Services. We are one of the nation's ten largest travel agencies. Because of the volume of business we have with all national carriers, the rates they offer us for customers like you and your husband are the lowest available. But, you may want to shop around. Check with your local agent. Then check with Sun Shine. You'll see the money we can save. But it's your choice, because these are your vacations."

"Roughly how much would the airfare be?"

"Ma'am, I have no way of knowing the price of the airfare for three reasons. From my computer, I have no access to the airlines' price schedule. Two, I don't know when during the year you and your husband will be taking the vacations. As I know you are aware, airline fares vary greatly by time of year. And, I don't know when during the next three years you and your husband will take the vacations. However, I do know that when you are ready to take your vacations, Sun Shine Travel Fight Services can offer you the lowest available fare."

"What costs will be my responsibility when we are on vacations?"

"Meals, other than the breakfasts at the Emperada, gasoline and insurance for the rental car, hotel room taxes and sales taxes on your purchases, port fees, and general spending money for your enjoyment. The rooms for ten nights, the rental car in the state of Florida, and the cruise to and from the Bahamas are all parts of your award."

"Now, we at Sun Shine Travel, would like to send you your complete vacation package including four-color brochures for each destination and resort, a video highlighting your trips, and your pre-authorized travel vouchers and itineraries to be completed when you make your reservations. Plus, because you called in this week, we are offering a special bonus. We will send to you valuable coupons for use at each resort . . . $300 worth of savings for excursions, meals and shopping.

We'd like to send your vacation package to Mrs. Estelle Brenton at 314 Rogers Court in Sioux Falls, South Dakota. When you receive the package you can sit with your husband and plan your vacations to suit your busy schedules. It takes approximately five working days for your vacation package to arrive by registered mail. We have to send it by registered mail, because it is so valuable. It contains the validated resort and travel vouchers and coupons. The total package has a retail value of over $2500. But, because you are an award winner, to secure your package so that you and your husband can make your plans, will require a fee of only $599. This can be applied to your credit card. Will that be Visa or MasterCard?"

"I thought I won the trips. It says here they are free."

"Ma'am, I'm sorry if there is confusion. But, the certificate, you received does say that you are entitled to the award. But, it does not say the vacations are free. The vacations are part of a promotion to introduce Sun Shine Travel Services to people like yourself. We are offering greatly discounted resort vacations. You'll take the vacations, appreciate the ease and luxury of traveling with us, use us again for other travel needs, and recommend us to friends.

It's like a store coupon for a box of detergent. You use the coupon, try the product, like the product, and become a steady and loyal customer. That's the way we build our business. And, we've been doing it this way for nine years. We know this method works because we offer great deals on great vacations. Now, will you be using Visa or MasterCard to secure your vacations?"

"I'm not payin' a thing 'til I talk to my husband. We make all big decisions together."

"That makes very good sense, ma'am. That's why we want to send you and your husband the complete package. The brochures, the video, the itineraries, the vouchers, the coupons . . . everything. That way you two can sit in the comfort of your own home and discuss how and when you will take the vacations. You'll have all the material in front of you so that you can make a good decision. We would not want to put you in the position of having to explain all the details of this very complete promotion, without having the material in front of you. Would you like to put the $599 on your American Express Card?"

"I would like to know what I'm spending the money for."

"Like I said, the promotion is like a store coupon. But, in stead of you paying 90% of the value of the item at the store, the fee covers the processing and handling costs, which amount to less than 25% of the total value. You are saving over 75% of the total price of the vacations. When the package, containing the pre-approved travel vouchers, itineraries, and coupons is mailed to you, it has an estimated retail value of $2,500 to $3,000. That's what these vacations would cost considering a total of ten nights at the luxury resorts and the discount coupons. But, because you are an award winner, you have the right to secure the vacations for the greatly reduced rate. This is our promotional discount to you. Just like the manufacturer discounts the price of the product you secure at the store. So, will that be Visa or MasterCard?"

"Let me get back to you after I talk to my husband. I took real good notes. Then, when he understands, and if he says it's all right, we'll call back."

"I'm sorry, ma'am. The certificate is clear on callbacks. In the center at the bottom of the face, you'll see the red words, One Call Per Award Winner. This has been your one call. That's why we want to send the complete package of material to you. You can review it with your husband and decide when you'll take your vacations.

Wait a minute. Something special just popped-up on my computer screen. I've not seen this before. Your certificate is truly special. You are a very lucky winner of the promotion; because these vacations are very unique . . . these vacations are transferable. That means once you have secured them with a major credit card you may give any one or all of them as a gift or gifts to your adult children. Or, even to a friend. You and your husband may want to take one trip and give two away. Maybe you know someone with small children who would like the Disney vacation. Then you and your husband can go to the Bahamas and Cancun. These vacations could be wonderful gifts. Very unique gifts you got at an unbelievable discount. Which card would you like to use?"

"Before I do anything I must find out if you are legitimate."

"Ma'am, it's always wise to be prudent. We like to help smart clients. Sun Shine Travel is one of the ten largest travel agencies in the U.S. We have been promoting our services with special vacation packages for more twelve years. We are members of the International Better Business Bureau, the local Chamber of Commerce, and we are regulated by the Florida Department of Commerce in Tallahassee. We are successful because we deliver what we promise.

If we ran promotions in which people didn't get what we promised, their word of mouth, not to mention lawsuits would have put us out of business long ago. The Department of Commerce would see to that. And, since we have been doing this for over a decade and since we are in the top ten, we must be legitimate. Plus, our practices can be checked with local, state, and international regulators. Now, I'd like to send the prepaid material out to you and your husband. Which credit card would you like to use?"

"Do you have any telephone numbers for the Better Business Bureau and the Florida Department of Commerce? I'd like to check your company out before I buy anything."

"Checking your purchase makes good sense, ma'am. Let me punch up those telephone numbers on my computer screen. The Better Business Bureau's Toll Free number is 1-888-438-7573. The number for the Florida Department of Commerce in Tallahassee, Florida is 1-351-456-7890, and then you'll hit extension 8632. After the next prompt, enter the code for Sun Shine Travel. That code is 4892. A voice will confirm the high quality of our business practices."

"Thank you. I'll call these numbers and get back to you."

"I'm sorry, ma'am. Once we hang up, if you have not secured your vacations with a credit card, the vacations will become part of our promotional treasure chest and made available to another award winner. If you chose not to secure the vacations with this call, I am required to re-enter the main frame and delete your name. This makes the vacations available to another award winner. However, we encourage you to call these numbers during working hours. You'll see that everything I told you about our business practices is true. Now, which card would you like to use? Visa?"

"Can I send the material back to you once my husband and I have looked at it?"

"Ma'am, why would you send the material back to us once it has been activated in your name?"

"Well, maybe there is something we don't like about it."

"What's not to like? Three great resorts. The freedom to take the vacations in any sequence and combination you choose. The freedom to take the vacations whenever you choose during the next three years. No blackout periods. A saving of over $2000 over the price of the resort stays. The freedom to give any part or all of the vacations as gifts. Would you like to put this on your American Express card or Visa?"

"Why not just send the material to us and if we like it, we'll charge it to our Visa?"

"Ma'am, I'm sorry. It would not be prudent business practices for us to send $3000 worth of activated travel vouchers and discount coupons worth over $3000 in the mail in the hopes that you might pay the promotional fee. The manufacturer, who sent you the coupon, chose not to send you the complete and full package of product for the same reason. The vacation vouchers will be pre-approved and can be used by anyone . . . you or a friend.

So, if you were to get the pre-approved vouchers and chose not to pay us, we would be about $2,500 in the hole. By sending the activated itineraries and pre-approved vouchers to you to look at without you paying the modest promotional fee, we are risking a great deal with little chance of reward. But, if you activate the vouchers and itineraries with you credit card, you are free to do with them what you wish."

"What happens if we pay for the trips, get the package and decide that we really don't want to take the vacations?"

"You can give any or all of them as gifts. But, wouldn't it be great to spend some quality time with your husband in a romantic tropical resort? Let me ask you. When was that last time you and your husband got away for a vacation? Got away to somewhere where you can relax, sleep in, nap on the beach, enjoy great meals, and maybe dance into the night. Get the romance juices flowing? This is your chance to do something special together. Give both of you the vacation you've always wanted. Will you be using your MasterCard?"

"But, what if he's upset that I went and did something this big without first talking it over with him? Then what do I do?"

"Do you really think he would be upset that you love him and that you wanted to do something special for him. If he is upset, which I highly doubt, then you can give the vacations as gifts. They would make great Christmas gifts. But I would hate to see you miss out on your dream vacations. Will that be Visa or MasterCard?"

"After we see the material . . . say we don't like it, how do we get our money back?"

"Credit card purchasing is the safest in the world. You use a credit card to protect you. The credit card has a contract with you. Not with us. The credit card works for you and will fight for you. If Sun Shine Travel didn't conduct business the way the credit cards require, we couldn't use them to help their clients. Sun Shine Travel and our business practices have been thoroughly reviewed by all the major credit cards . . . MasterCard, Visa, American Express, and Discover. They all have found that we are reputable and that we treat their clients honestly. That is, we deliver on our promotional promises. The four major credit cards approve of the way we do business. So you can rest assured that you can use your credit card with complete safety. Would you prefer to use Visa or Master Card?"

"You say that once I have paid for these vacations, if I don't like them I can cancel them through my credit card. How long will that take?"

"Depending on the card, the value of the resort vacation would be deleted from your card before the next billing cycle. So, you have the maximum protection."

"And, once I've paid for the vacations, if I can't use them for whatever reason, I can give them to anyone I wish."

"Yes, ma'am, that is correct. They are fully transferable to other adults, once the vacations have been secured by you. Would you like to use your Visa card?"

"I don't know. I'm going to have to discuss this with my husband and get back to you."

"While I applaud your judgement, I must remind you that the certificate clearly states that there is one call per winner. This is your one call. I think discussing the material with your husband is wise. That's why we want to send you the video and all the brochures. So both of you can see just how wonderful these resorts are. Ten nights, three resorts, a cruise, and a car rental. A retail value of nearly $3,000. Yours for less than $600. Because we are promoting our travel service with the hopes that Sun Shine will become your regular travel agency. Does your Visa start with a 4?"

"Wait a minute, I'm not charging anything this large to my Visa without talking to my husband first."

"Ma'am all the material and pre-approved vouchers to review in the comfort of your own home. An incredible bargain. Fully transferable. Credit card protection. You really have nothing to risk, now do you. Let us send the package to you and your husband. I guarantee you'll be glad you secured the vacations."

"Well . . . ."

Silence at my end forces her to tell me how to overcome her objection.

"What's troubling you, ma'am?"

"It's just that I've never bought anything this expensive without talking to my husband."

"Ma'am, it would like buying him a big easy chair for Christmas. You know one of the reclining kinds? Would you discuss the surprise gift with him before you bought it? Or would you buy it knowing he would love it, because he loves you?"

"But, what if he doesn't like the vacations? We'll be stuck with them."

"Ma'am, if you bought the reclining chair for him for Christmas, and for some strange reason he hated it, the store would take it back, wouldn't they?"

"Yes."

"If you bought the chair from a catalogue, they would take it back and give you a credit on your credit card, wouldn't they? Remember the credit card works for you. Not for us. It helps you if you change your mind."

"Yes."

"This vacation promotion is the same thing. We know that when you see all the material for the vacations, you and your husband will love them. Now, let's send you the complete package. It'll take about a week for the package to arrive. Inside the package will be a special 800 number you can call with any questions . . . dates or whatever. Now, what is your Visa account number?"

"Well, if you're sure this is safe. I mean I am protected by my Visa card. And we can take the vacations whenever we want."

"You are protected and there are no blackout periods."

Always through in an extra benefit when overcoming an objection

"Let me go to my purse and get my card."

Click! The sound of failure.

The fish flopped off the hook. She teased the fisherman, got scared, and wiggled off the hook. This is a downer. A defeat. No control. To be strung along with all the indications that my best work will prevail. My half-truths will be believed. Only to have the fish flop. Can't dwell on the failure of the past. Look for the success of the next call. Time for a cup of hemlock, but coffee will have to do. Back to the telephone.

* * *

"Why sure you can take these vacations when ever you want. There are no blackout periods. Bring the children to Disney World over the Christmas holiday. What a great gift for the entire family. No problem with making reservations. No blackout period. Just give us 90 days notice and you're playing with Mickey and Minnie.

Well the Silver Sands is a luxury villa-style resort. Every villa has a porch or balcony that opens out to the sea. Everyday you are wafted by the breezes off the ocean. The beaches are almost snow white. Plus, the marina has boats you can rent if you wish to take a luxurious sail in the lagoon. There is a continental breakfast served in the lobby every day. Downtown is about a ten-minute walk. Steel bands every night on the patio. Just sit and relax to the sounds of the tropics."

"If you like to party, Cancun will be the place for you. The Posada Laguna has its own private beach with volleyball nets and a huge Tiki bar. There are wave runners and sailing skiffs if you really want to have fun. I remember when my fiancée and were there. We got hooked on wave runners. Bought two when we got home. We're out on the bay or gulf every weekend. Unbelievable. You'll want to have at least one when you get back to Grand Rapids. Now . . .

The Big Red Boat is a true luxury liner. Five levels. Huge fore and aft decks for swimming and sunning. Three casinos set the right mood for your stay at the Silver Sands. The Silver Sands has one of the largest casinos on the island. And, as a winner of this Award from Sun Shine Travel, we provide you with a certificate redeemable in the casino. This certificate is worth $100 dollars in chips. Free gambling. You lose nothing and whatever you win is yours to keep. You can use them at anytime during your stay, but only at the Silver Sands.

The Posada Laguna is one of the hidden treasures of Cancun. It's medium size, but with all the amenities of the places further down on the beach. You'll get personal attention from a professional staff. Your every wish is their command.

Now we'd like to send this complete pre-approved package out to you in Ann Arbor. The package contains two videos, brochures, your own private Sun Shine Travel ID card, the pre-authorized vouchers and itineraries, $500 worth of coupons and a special 800 number you can call with any questions. This package has a retail value of over $3,000. But, because it is part of our Spring Promotion, and because your name is listed as an Award winner, the complete package can be secured for $599. Will you be using Visa or MasterCard?"

"I don't know . . ."

"There is really nothing to risk. The package comes to you via registered mail so delivery is safe. The vouchers and itineraries are in your name, yet they are fully transferable. They are yours to with as you please. That's great flexibility. Take the time to discuss this amazing award with your husband. Then decide when and where you will be going first. Would you like to secure this vacation award with your American Express card?"

"I'm not sure. I want to see all the details. Then I'll decide."

"Unfortunately we can't send an award package with pre-approved and pre-authorized travel vouchers worth in excess of $2,250 in the mail just for you to look at. This is a special promotion offer. It works like a store coupon. You use the coupon to try the product. And, because it's a good product, you become a loyal customer. But, it's better than a coupon, because you will not be responsible for 95% of the total retail value. You can secure these vacations for less than 20% of the total retail value.

We do this, be cause after traveling to these three destinations, we know that you will appreciate your vacations and want to use our other travel services in the future. That's why we can offer you a package worth over $2,250 for less than $600. We want to be your travel agent for a long time. Will you be using your Visa card to secure your vacations?

You are fully protected by your credit card. Remember that we could not offer you the freedom to use your credit card if your credit card did not approve what we offer and how we do business. You use MasterCard right? Well, the MasterCard people come to our offices and observe how we conduct twice a year. They inspect the vacation resorts. Then, and only then, they give us the right to accept their clients' cards. If MasterCard didn't approve of this promotion, we could not take your card. Now, your MasterCard starts with a 5 . . ."

"This makes me nervous."

"What can you be afraid of? What did you buy your husband for Christmas last year? A big screen TV for the den. Hey, I wish my wife were so generous. I got a dress shirt and a floating Styrofoam chair for the pool. But, I'll bet you spent over $1000 for the big screen TV. And you did that without asking his permission. Did you charge it on a store account or did you charge your Visa card. Your Discover card, I see. So you took some time to pay off the gift. Well, that's the way to look at these great vacation bargains.

For less than $600 you can give your husband and yourself the gift of a lifetime. Something you two can share and have memories for ever. If you took the trip next winter, when the snow is at your door, the vacation would already be paid for. No lingering debt. Just a great vacation free and clear. And, for a lot less than the big screen TV. Your Discover card begins with a 6 . . .

But it's your card, am I right? What I'm hearing, and correct me if I'm wrong, is that your husband won't let you charge anything on your card that he hasn't approved of in advance although you are responsible for the card and the payments. Am I right? Of course, you want to discuss this with your husband. I understand that. I completely endorse that.

It's the same with my wife and me. We discuss every major purchase and every major event. But, I trust my wife to make well thought out decisions. I trust my wife to ask my opinion not my permission when she does something big. Now, I want my children to ask my permission, because I am financially responsible for them. But, my wife has her own job just like you. She makes good money just like you. We jointly run the house and raise the children, but each of us trusts the other enough that we can and do some things on our own. I go fishing on the gulf with my buddies. She goes shopping with her buddies. We each spend our own money. Can you do that? Spend your own money?"

"Can I trust you?"

"We could not be in business for fifteen years, if we didn't deliver the vacations that people secure. If we didn't have many satisfied customers.

Your MasterCard starts with a 5 . . ."

I look at the board. The harvest from the sea has been flimsy today. As it was yesterday and Monday. The mailing for leads is the problem. No one on the board has more than two hits and everybody has *deeks*, or declines. The caller wants to be sold and has a credit card. But the card just doesn't have a high enough limit or doesn't have enough left on the limit to accept the $599 charge. The fish are out there. They're just too scrawny. This is the most frustrating time to be a telehuckster. Work, cajole, plead, and intimidate. Most people just hang up. The ones that don't are too proud to admit they can't afford the vacations.

It's going to be a shitty week. I can see it in the eyes of the dayshift. They're scared. Scared of not meeting quota. Scared of the shift supervisor berating them in front of their peers. Scared of not making enough money to pay for the drugs, booze, or their part of the communal rent. Fear of failure drives these people to lie more outrageously than normal. They make promises that would get them in trouble with the State Attorney General. And we all know that people from that office are listening to what we say and how we say it. If they catch one of us . . . or when they catch one of us . . . making a lie to make a sale, we can be dismissed and the company fined. Too many transgressions and the company will be put out of business.

That's why the shift supervisor paces around the room listening into our conversations, standing over our shoulders, pointing to our rebuttal book, and commanding us to close, close, close. Push until the caller either gives it up or hangs up. The quota is 4-6 calls each hour. Fewer calls if the callers show even vague interest and require cajoling. More calls if the callers sense what is happening and hang up early. We can take a break at the end of each hour, if we have met our quota and if there are no calls in queue.

The day shift manager is a wiry woman named Celia. She looks and acts like a Bantam Rooster. Very colorful. She is over-dressed and wears too much make-up. She struts. She crows. If, we can't close, she will jump on our phones to show us how it is done. She does this for three reasons. First to train us. Second to humble us. Third to earn the override. Just once have I seen her fail to close. Some slick Willie hung up on her. Celia claimed that no one could have closed that son-of-a-bitch. She was right.

There is no set method to sell. The key is to get inside the caller's head. Present the bait as truly desirable. Tell the caller what he wants to hear. This is the tough part. The telemarketer must get inside the caller's head within the first sixty seconds of the call. The telemarketer must understand age, life style, aspirations and, most of all, the size of the caller's ego. Should the man or woman be brow beaten? Intimidated? Seduced? Humiliated? Or must the telemarketer build up the caller's ego? Pump it up. Create a superhero. Then con the caller into making his own decision. The only decision. The decision to buy. Once the ground rules are established, the telemarketer sets about to land the fish . . . casts his line with the proper bait and the hook hidden. He knows when the fish is hooked. What he doesn't know is precisely how to reel in the fish. Should the line be tugged hard so that the hook digs deeply into the jaw? Will that cause so much pain that the fish will risk injury to escape?

Or, should the line be drawn ever so slightly until the fisherman can feel the tension as the fish nibbles? Then the line is let out so that the fish loses sight of the bait and comes back for a bigger bite. The line is drawn in. Let out. Drawn in. Let out. Finally the fish, weary of the game, takes a huge bite and swallows the bait and the hook. He is caught, but he thought it was his own doing. Fish are so fucking stupid.

There more personalities on this end of the telephone than a building full of schizophrenics. Grandmother. Grandfather. Uncle. Aunt. Hot shot. Girl next door. Boy next door. Father. Mother. Sister. Brother. Bully. School chum. Expert. Joe casual. Slow wit. Stutterer. Happy go lucky . . . male and female. Exuberant youth. Sage. Seductress and seducer. Struggling parent. Been-there-done-that smart-ass. Devil-may-care. Self-assured. Self-conflicting.

Plus, there are accents and dialects created to mirror the caller. Establish camaraderie. Kinship. Break down the barrier of suspicion and disguise the bait. Irish immigrant. Redneck. Southern belle and gentleman. English sophisticate. Midwest farmer. New York City regular. New Englander. Southwest cowboy or girl.

Some even use the approach of opposites. Be nothing like the caller. Draw the caller out. Make him an expert. Inflate the sense of self worth. Get the caller to talk about his world from the standpoint of a teacher. The telehuckster is just a student at the master's feet. As the master teaches, he begins to appreciate the willingness of the student. This appreciation turns to trust. Trust turns to a sale.

All of this conniving, deception, and trickery is for the sole purpose of earning money per sale. The expression, "Whatever it takes", truly and accurately defines telemarketing.

III

The week's black promise has been delivered. The sales are few and far between. There have been more *deeks* than sales on the board each shift each day. Five day shifts have garnered thirty-six sales. And the night shift is not much better than the day. Most of the people on the day shift have four sales. That's not even minimum wage for the week. All of the angst. All of the fear. For next to nothing. They are talking about drinking their failures away on Friday night. I am not much better off.

Jimmy and Della each have ten. They must be pitching real heat. Promising that the amount won't hit the credit card until after the package has arrived and been reviewed. Promising out right that the caller can cancel the purchase and return the material at anytime. These are definite "no-nos". We can allude to the credit card cancellation mechanics, but never promise them directly. Promising them directly gives the caller the mind-set that he is truly risking nothing. That he is in control. He is never in control until he hangs up.

The sale must go through and hold. The caller must not cancel the purchase. He can't even think he can cancel. He must be deluded into the false sense of well being that he has nothing to lose. He can transfer. But, he must buy first. If he tries to cancel the package after receipt, the operators on the "Special 800 Service Line" will convince him that it is in his best interest to keep the vacation vouchers and itineraries. Give them the three useless trips as gifts. These operators get paid for saves. They work extra hard.

Maybe tomorrow will be better. It has to be better. I need a triple just to pay my rent and take care of basics the week after next. The good news is that this payday will be for fourteen deals. The bad news is that all of them will show up on the paycheck. Big taxes. No special cash incentive. Better put as much aside as possible for the upcoming drought. That's the bitch of telemarketing. Pay is variable and week-to-week. Bills are fixed and month-to-month.

The night shift manager is a young guy . . . Pete. He speaks Spanish to those callers who feel more comfortable dealing with one of their own. Another con. He keeps all the Spanish sales. Plus, he gets an override from the rest of us. Last week was great for Pete. This week is not so good. He pushes us to close, close, close, close, because his mortgage payment depends on our success. Pete knows that I will be working tomorrow, so he lets me clock out a little early. The guys who won't be working tomorrow will close down. That takes at least an hour after the phones are turned off. Insert my time card into the clock. I head for the parking lot.

* * *

In the corner of the lot away from the office entrance there are two cars parked one behind the other with their parking lights and motors on. The cars are about forty feet from my trusty steed. I notice four guys standing near the open trunk of the front car. The trunk light shines upon their dark and surly countenances. Two of them are leaning into the trunk. As I insert the key into the driver's door. The voices of the four guys become audible. They are arguing. They are screaming. Then pop, pop, pop, pop, pop. Shots.

More screaming. Rage mixed with pain. Turn my head to catch the action and I see the four guys shooting at each other. Two on the ground and two by the trunk. The car, parked to the rear, revs its engine and roars toward me. Tires screeching as a dark colored four-door General Motors product roars passed me.

The driver's window is down and I see the profile of a male with a long moustache, shoulder length hair, a Mediterranean nose, and a round silver stud in his left ear. What I got was one of those flash bulb glimpses. Almost subliminal, but all the details are obvious and stay with me. The car leaps from the parking lot, and screeches onto the side road leading to the interstate. From staring at the rear lights and the lit undercarriage, I turn to the remaining car and the four guys. Pop. The burn in my thigh is real. The impact of the hit and the pain cause me to stagger backward. Now, I'm pissed. I've done nothing to warrant being a target. I limp to the car and the men.

One of the guys on the ground is very still. I guess he is very dead. He has no head from his eyebrows north. Consequently his face is unrecognizable. The second guy is flopping like a fish on the deck. He can't speak, but he gurgles in rage. He has two visible wounds. One in his stomach and one in his chest. He is pointing his gun in my vague direction. He will try to finish what his first shot failed to accomplish. His eyes are clouded by tears. His gun hand is aiming anywhere as if it has a mind of its own. I rush to him.

Standing over him, I apply my right Bass Wejun to his neck and stand on that foot. The crunching sound of breaking trachea, the small neck bones, and cartilage is complemented by the gurgling and gasping that comes through his mouth from the hole in his lungs. Blood erupts from his nose and mouth. It splatters on my shoe. His eyeballs bug out like those of a Lemur. He endures a series of violent spasms before he slumps into never. I have no idea who this would-be killer is or was.

"Fuck you, cockroach."

The two guys at the trunk have not moved since I got to the car. Leaning into the cavernous rear compartment, I see why. Their bodies look like human punchboards. Holes all over and blood oozing from each inflicted aperture. The lights in the trunk reveal the pools of blood and three airline bags with shoulder straps. Bag number one contains hundreds and hundreds of small plastic packets fill with white powder. Bag number two, the same. Bag number three is loaded with cash. Twenties, fifties and hundreds. Four dead guys and the booty from a drug deal gone bad. Mine, the cops, or the dealers. I make a management decision. Mine. All three bags are dumped into my trunk. I head back to the office.

Once on 911 I explain I have been witness to a shooting in the parking lot. I have been shot. There were two cars. Four guys remain in the parking lot. One guy and one car escaped. The police arrive in five minutes. After brief questioning, I am taken to the hospital for treatment of the gunshot wound. The wound is not life threatening. Flesh and muscle torn. No cartilage or ligament damage. The bullet passed right through the outer portion of my thigh. The nurse washes the two holes and gives me a shot. No stitches. Just two small butterfly bandages and a wrap.

Antibiotics, some strong painkillers, and a cane. I promise to hobble back for a check-up in three days, and indulge no strenuous activity. The cops have my name, address, telephone number and where to reach me during the day. I am an unfortunate bystander to a crime scene. They drive me from the hospital to my car and follow me to make sure I get to my residence.

I can't sleep. It's like Christmas Eve . . . looking at all the gifts. The bounty in the bags must be examined. There must be the better part of a kilo in each of the drug bags. Neatly broken down into saleable packets. No telling how often the shit has been stepped on. I'll have to sample the merchandise tomorrow before work. Can't miss work. Can't do anything out of the ordinary. Besides I'm somewhere between a hero and a victim. Great story to tell over and over and over again. Get some sympathy. Maybe get a sympathy fuck out of it from Terri. She's been flirting with me since her husband left. Now is the time for her to put out or shut up.

Bag number three is a cash trove. A total of $8,200 in unmarked untraceable street cash. All mine. The big score just got bigger. Three questions. How to dispose of the coke? What to do with money? Where to stash the bags? I need a drink. The booze and the pain meds will put me to sleep. I'll solve the hydra-question tomorrow.

The newspaper and the early TV news carry major stories about the murders in "a suburban strip mall parking lot." No mention of me, the drugs, or the money. The apparent motive is "a gang assassination." "There were no witnesses." This is the latest in "the rising tide of gang violence." Ethnic gangs fighting each other. "Turf wars over extortion, prostitution, gambling, legitimate and otherwise, and drug distribution."

The Saturday shift is noon to six. I make it on time. The throbbing in my leg is obvious to me, but not debilitating. The coke was a B+. Strong enough to get me to the phones and push me for two hours. I'll finish the last of the packet at break. Maybe I can sell it $80 a gram. Not on the streets. Sell in the bars or at the parties of the Yuppies. A few grams at a time. Do not arouse suspicion of either the police or the original owner. Particularly the latter.

* * *

First call of the day. Some idiot in Minot. He and his wife wanted the free vacations sent overnight so they could use them in two weeks. He got pissed about the second request for his card. Could not understand how something free could cost him $599. Hung up on the third request for his card. No sales on the board by 1:30. Three *deeks*. Lots of calls in queue. Given the shitty list, we must work especially hard just to be rejected. But, we can't waste time on dead beats. Bad list yet screaming pressure from Celia. Rock and hard place. Sisyphus had more fun, but he had no jack.

Finally, a sale. Grandmother in Omaha. She wants to give the vacations as gifts. I became her child with a child of my own . . . her grandson. I seduced the old lady and got into her financial panties. It's now 4:30 and I feel I have my deal for the day. One of three on the board. Fifteen *deeks*. The group is complaining about the list. Can't sell to the poor and the dead. We are pushed harder. Tension is visible in the room. Clouding sales judgement. Half the people dump at the first sign of caller stupidity. They frantically jump to the next caller, who is softened by the sales message on hold.

The other group patiently, even maniacally, works each call. Spending a lot of time in the hopes of a partial. If the card holds at least one half of the amount, the huckster gets $15. The commission balance is paid when the fish sends a check or calls back with a second credit card. All of that must occur within two working days. At least that's what we tell the fish. This week, we will do anything for a sale. Even a partial.

The totals for Saturday: 273 incoming, 31 *deeks*, 8 full sales, and 3 partials. Pathetic. Uneasiness has given way to anger. The sales people have been screwed over by the list people. We will be blamed for the overall failure. Weeks like this that can kill a room. People leave. New people have to be trained. That's time, money, and an unproductive learning curve. The company policy about missing quota for two straight weeks does not apply to weeks like this when no one can make quota. But, the policy is simple.

If someone misses quota for two straight weeks of decent lists, he or she is put on probation, retrained and very closely monitored for the next week. If, after the reprogramming week, the person misses quota a third time, while most others are making their nut, the poor schlub is fired. This process weeds out the weak and destroys many of them in the process. Celia promises next week will be better. The mailings that started Friday were directed to an upper-middle income target in the Southwest. Think cowboy next week and you'll get more than your quota. Beer and pizza for the crew. We wait in line for our picnic payoff. Food and drink are inhaled by everyone. Only empty boxes, a few pizza bones, and crushed cans are visible after twenty minutes. The company fills our stomachs with warm food and softens our anger with alcohol in an effort to placate us in the face of failure. Every con can be conned. Terri's husband came back.

* * *

"What's shaken tonight oh wounded soldier?"

"Jimmy, I think I'll go to Chili's, eat free bar food, get drunk, and let some lonely woman take advantage of me for hours on end at her place."

"We're cruisin'. Stop by Chili's later to catch your act."

On my bed is displayed my economic salvation. The second half of the gram snorted at the office is rushing through my body. I can't relax. So, I count. Stack. Re-count and re-stack. The packets and the bills. They must be hidden. Somewhere that only I can access and that I can access easily. A bin at the nearby U-Stor-It fits those criteria. Maybe they have small bins. Pull out twenty packets and $200. Break down the remainder into piles of twenty packets and place these in triple ziplock bags . . . inside a sealed kitchen garbage bag . . . inside the airline bags. Humidity can turn my cache into valueless clumps of clay. There is no need to rewrap the money. It won't spoil.

U-Stor-It is located about two miles from my room and notes three sizes of bins and twenty-four hour access. I take a small, personal bin farther from the gate. For the six-month-paid-in-advance fee, I receive my own pass code to the Storage Park. The code, when entered onto the keypad, opens the gate. I supply my own lock and keep the key. They will not take an extra key. The bin is about twenty times larger than I need for the three bags, but it's the smallest they have. I'll have to buy some stuff to store in the bin . . . a bicycle and some empty boxes. Disguise the real booty. The goody bags are stashed inside a carton, wrapped in a tied lawn and leaf bag. Home to shower and shave. Off to Chili's. I have to be careful not to get my bandage wet in the shower. The throbbing has subsided. Managing with the cane is easier than I had thought. I even look slightly mysterious and sophisticated.

Ten o'clock. About time for the last drink and to head home. Into the bar come two women in jeans, western shirts, and cowboy boots. The race track season is in its last week. Over the next six days there are six major races. The money draws everyone. The last of the snowbird tourists, the trainers and owners of second-rate ponies, and the combines looking to buy animals. The recent bar entrants fit somewhere in that expansive population. I start to move so they can sit together at the bard, but they sit on either side of me.

"Long day?"

"About eighteen hours so far. We were going to head home tonight, but decided to flop in a motel nearby and drive back to Dothan tomorrow. Deserve a drink first."

"Allow me."

"Two Jacks straight up. Thank you."

The three of us sit for a moment. Each waiting for one of the other to continue the verbal probing. The blonde breaks the silence.

"Do you know how we can get to the Holiday Inn on Tresvant Road?"

"Sure. When you leave this parking lot, hang a right and go . . . let me see . . . four traffic lights. That's about two miles. Take a left onto Broadmeer Boulevard. There is a Wendy's and an Exxon station on your left. Turn there and go three lights. That's about five miles, maybe a little more. You'll see two churches at that intersection. Turn right. The Holiday Inn will be about four miles on your right. Got that."

The brunette looks puzzled.

"Not really. Could you write those directions down on this napkin?"

"Sure. Another round?"

"Yeah, thanks. You're being very generous."

"I had a good week and love sharing with lovely ladies."

Written directions and a mini map all on one napkin. Da Vinci would be in awe. I stand between the two women and go over every point of the directions. I brush up against the blonde's left shoulder and the brunette's right. As we focus on the napkin in the dimly lit bar, I feel the pressure of breasts on both my arms. The coke, alcohol, and sexual electricity spin my mind. My fantasy is interrupted by the bartender's last call. Pay up and head for the door followed by my two newfound friends.

"I am lousy at following a map. Could you do us a big favor and lead us over to the Holiday Inn. I mean if it's not too far out of your way or anything. We're hauling this horse trailer and making cross traffic turns can be a real pain. We'd appreciate it."

"Sure, be glad to help."

* * *

The two-vehicle caravan makes the trip in thirty-five minutes. As we pull into the parking lot, the brunette bounds from the cab of the truck. And prances to my window.

"You want to join us for a night cap. Our treat."

"How can I say no?"

"Wait for us to register."

In less than twenty minutes the two of them exit the lobby, wave for me to follow them and then go around the corner to the back lot.

"Our room is 326. We have a bottle. There'll be glasses in the room. We're ready if you are."

The anticipation is staggering. It overcomes the awkwardness of climbing stairs with my cane. I arrive at the room about three minutes after they enter. The room looks like every other Holiday Inn room I've ever been in. Immediately I notice a packet with white powder, a cut-off straw, and a hand mirror on the bedside table. The blonde begins scraping lines.

"We don't have much, but you're welcome to share."

"I have some. Let's all share."

I hand her my packet. Small like hers. She creates six three-inch white trails of happiness. One for each nostril in the room.

"Your stuff is really primo. Would you know where we could get more?"

"I got this from a buddy at work. I could ask him."

"Make yourself comfortable. We need to shower. Desperately need to shower. Care to join us?"

I am out of my clothes and into the steamy bathroom about one minute after the lathering starts. Three soapy bodies in a space built for one. Squeezing against each other to form a three-mouthed, three-crotched, six-handed mass of kissing, fondling, licking humanity. The suds mingle with the sweat of the day, the chlorine laced public utility water, and the musk of primal urges. The water is hot . . . very hot. My eyes close, I am swimming in a fantasy realized. I sway to the ebb and flow of their horizontal and vertical tides. Cleaned, excited, and rinsed, I am led to the bed and told to lie on my back.

Immediately, I am covered with more kissing and licking. Now there is a sense of urgency to the stimulation. With the ease of experience, the two silent bodies mount me. I am the means to their ends. The grinding starts ever so gradually and builds to syncopation . . . one up . . . one down. Rising and steadily lowering, the pressure points of their bodies come to rest on the targets of their desires. I am an inanimate object. The two derive pleasure from themselves and me. Their breathing has become deep and audible. Moans begin. Four hands now grip me . . . two on the shoulders and two on the hips. The hands are released and I see the two are holding each other's shoulders. The two bodies are rising, falling and grinding. Moans are at a conversational level.

"Bitch."

"Whore."

"I love you."

"I love you, too, bitch."

I am not sure I heard a slap. But, I am aware of a mild scrap above me. Soft slaps, hair pulling, biting, and scratching. They are beginning to go into spasms of very physical ecstasy. I am literally along for the ride. Just a toy to get them to the point where they could get off. The words are unrecognizable, as mouths are locked in the final moment.

Collapse. They are done. Not me. They slide to the same side of the human pleasure bench and cradle each other. I do not exist. My manhood is to no avail. The breathing beside me is delicate and as from one body. They sleep.

I rise and dress. My wallet is not in the right rear pocket, but on the night table. I exit stage right. All the way home and as I am falling asleep the same question; *What the fuck just happened?*

* * *

Sunday is my day with my boy. Just guys: one eleven and one much older. It's difficult to know what David wants to do during our one regular day, because it is just one of seven. I have to work hard to understand his feelings and his hopes for us, as well as the day. I hope for a full day so he is not bored. Some events are planned and some are spontaneous. At least one new thing each Sunday to expand his awareness and probe for areas of interest. We don't go to my room. There's nothing to do there and I am ashamed. Maybe I compensate by planning too thoroughly.

Reading the Sunday papers and having a big breakfast gives us a chance to talk about the week, as well as what is in the news. Sports news. Pour over the help wanted classifieds. Send at least two resumes per week to blind sales and marketing leads. Save the Op-ed section for my late night reading. Off to the beach for a long walk, sea glass collecting, and philosophical conversation. This week the walk is difficult for me. But I manage.

Green and brown from beer bottles are no big deal. But, any blue or red is to be cherished. David has a few of these special pieces. We talk about his school, buddies, and hopes for high school sports. No girl friends yet. Normally, we go to the basketball courts for a one-on-one. Not today. We spend the daylight hours outside. The fresh air is a wonderful tonic for my hangover, and the walking helps the healing. An early dinner and movie. We hold hands. I love him so.

As much as I want to I can't tell him about being conquered last night. He's not old enough to understand locker room talk or the thrill of this all-male fantasy. I can't tell him of my recent windfall or the circumstances around it either. I tell him I tripped on a curb and fell on my thigh. Big, deep bruise requires the cane. The illegality of the money and the coke is just not appropriate for him. Plus, some of the information would wash back to his mother, who needs to nothing of my good fortune.

Leaving him to get out of the marriage was like leaving my right arm in a trap to escape the bear. There are so many things I want to ask him and tell him, but to ensure his trust I must remain calm and cool. Something his mother has never been. He knows that I will never be too far away. And he has my pager number. Our code is 4852#. He can call me on my cell phone. This must be very discreet, because his mother does not know that I have a phone . . . just the beeper. When I get back on my feet financially and have an appropriate place, he can come and stay for a few days at a time. My big score will make that happen.

* * *

That evening at my place I do my best Bartelby Scrivener. From a Brooks Brothers shoebox I retrieve all the bills and past due notices, which are my obsession. On four sheets of yellow paper I carefully write all my debts. Gross and monthly payments. Feds, creditors, doctors, educators, and retailers. On two sheets the debts are listed in alphabetical order. On two sheets the debts are listed hierarchically by amount. The exact amounts are listed based upon the most recent bill or dunning letter. There is no rounding up or down. On a fifth sheet I itemize all monthly expenditures beyond debts . . . reduced alimony and child support, rent, food, gasoline, laundry, car insurance, etc. for the last three months. On a sixth sheet I write my weekly reported net income for the past three months. Thirteen entries.

I compare my average monthly income (4.33 x my average weekly paycheck) to the total of the monthly debt payments and expenditures. I already had an idea the answer should be written in red ink. I am depressed to see how much red was necessary. If my calculations are correct I am $626.47 short each month. Thank god for the A/B pay schedule. I can almost live, if I hit big on the B weeks, make partial payments, live frugally, not get injured, keep the car from major repairs, and nothing befalls David. But, I have no future except this bleak marginal economic existence until all the debts are dramatically reduced or I increase my income. Before the three-bag bounty that looked like two years. After all the debt is paid, I get to pay for a better living. Twenty-four months in this self-made fiscal prison before the American dream of debt from living well.

But, the recent three-bags-for-one-bullet trade gives me two ways out. One immediate. One gradual. I can take the cash and pay off some debts. Leave a little for emergencies. No treats. Then I can sell-off the grams of coke over the next year or so to create my new and better life. Can't unload all of the coke at once. I can make my money being an invisible supplier. Stay off the three sonar screens; the police, my Ex, and the former owner of my booty.

Which debts to attack? I must be judicious. Payments must go to those people who will accept cash. Whether they report the cash is their own business. I want my name off their books. No more dunning letters or letters from them or collection agencies. I can only pay off one or two creditors at a month. No real big splash of cash. First will be David's school and two doctors. Month three, I'll pay the dentist and three department stores. Plus, I'll make a double payment each month to the thieves that are holding the refinance note on my car. Prepay the car insurance with an untraceable money order and spend whatever it costs to get the car in to safe shape. A new car will have to wait for at least eighteen months. A new car would be a display of sudden wealth.

I am like a drunken soldier at payday. I want to spend until there is no more. The soldier derives pleasure from his spending. Booze and hookers. My pleasure is derived from controlling and eliminating my debt. When I have money, money works for me. When I don't, I work for money. When I have money, debt can be controlled. When I don't, debt controls me. Like right now. There is a line, which I have crossed from time to time. Not a time line or a foul line, it is a debt line. When I had a job and money I thought I could always get back to the safe side of the debt line. When I had a job and money, I lived well, and incurred debt. It's the American way. I managed to have a great deal of fun. Debt provides the trappings of fun.

But, when I lost my job and income, my life-style and debt didn't change immediately. They are components of a snowball I had been pushing down hill. The harder I pushed during the good times, the faster the snowball rolled and the larger it got. It was fun. It was a drug. I was in control or so I think. Suddenly I lost control. I had no steady income. But, the snowball didn't stop rolling. In fact it accelerated down hill gathering mass. I had to catch up to this runaway mass and regain control of it. But, I slipped and fell time and time again. As an unemployed, I fell more than when I was employed. That's a universal fact. I was responsible for the snowball, but couldn't control it. Now I have a chance to control it . . . to melt the snowball and owe nothing to nobody. That's my American fantasy. Debt free. That's me.

By those who do not know the true measure of a man, he is defined by money. On the low rungs on the economic ladder, the definition is based on cash. On the higher rungs, the definition is based on wealth. The system is a constant although the measurement values change. From folded green in the right pants pocket, to gold credit cards, to amounts on monthly statements paid by accountants. If a man has it, others know it. These are peers. The wad of cash on Friday night confirms value just as much as never carrying a wallet. If a man doesn't have it, everybody knows and his fear of their reactions eats at his soul. Now I have it, but I can't show and tell. I can't tell all those who doubted me that I am back. Back with a vengeance. The agony of the ecstasy. All of this mental masturbation, the full day with David, and the activity of last night cause me to collapse on top of the yellow lined paper.

I spring out of bed eager to make payments and start my return to responsible adult financial life. After the shower I remove the bullet wound bandage, the vestige of my part in the trade. The blood and other fluid are dried, so I wash the wound. Grab my wooden appendage and head to my personal bank then off to the first debt. The school was surprised to be paid in cash, while to the office managers at the doctors it was business as usual. By two I have completed my rounds, done some food shopping, and taken my car to a local repair shop for an estimate of what is needed to make it safe and what is needed to make it pleasant. Brakes, rotors, front wheel suspension, new tires, balance and alignment, an electrical tune-up, air conditioning compressor, battery, all new belts and an alternator. Total: $1,745 and four days. I'll need to rent a car for that time. That's another $150. Hate to, but must do it this way. Drop off next Tuesday.

* * *

Time to be a cowboy, baby. The board is alive with deals and a few *deeks*. This is a hot list. Better get more than my share. First three calls are losers. They hang up before I can tell them about Cancun. Caller number four is hooked and has a good card. One deal an hour for six hours would earn me a bonus of $100 at the end of the shift. Paid in cash. My second-hour deal takes over 22 minutes to close. Five rebuttals and the couple very reluctantly gives up their Visa. This one may kick by the end of the week. Six calls into the third hour and I score again. A young man plans to use the full trip as his honeymoon next March. My pager buzzes. Not David or the witch. I call the number.

"Officer Willow speaking. How may I help you?"

"Officer Willow, this is David Kermasic. I believe you paged me."

"Yes, sir. Thanks for getting right back to me. I'm doing follow-up into the shooting you witnessed last Friday. I would like to talk to you some more to amplify and clarify some details and dig into other areas in the crime scene reports. When would it be convenient for you to come down to the station?"

"Well, I work from 4 to 10 PM. Anytime before three. How about tomorrow?"

"Tomorrow is fine, sir. How about 10 AM?"

"That's fine."

"See you tomorrow down here at the central station. Thanks again, Mr. Kermasic."

Now what do they really want? Undoubtedly, they will try to find some inconsistency in my account. They'll try to trip me up. Maybe I saw something that I don't want them to know about. Be cool.

The deals stop. I am not focussed on closing. The call from the cops has distracted me. Lost control. I am thinking about my situation and can't get into the heads of the callers. Can't connect. Can't get the cards. Fuck it. Three for the night is good. Bobby got the $100. I wonder how many will hold. Terri got five deals. She can focus now that she is part of a couple again. Sally got four *deeks*. She has been complaining that telemarketing may not be for her. If she continues this dead streak. Her dreams of failure will be fulfilled.

The police station is a testament to the excess of political patronage. Completed two years ago, this five-story complex covers three city blocks. It has everything the PD needs to function from an auto repair shop to the morgue, from a firing range to the forensic lab. Enough parking for all the civilian vehicles, including guests. Two Urban Assault Vehicles hidden in an underground vault. A warehouse with a hidden entrance contains every conceivable weapon. Everybody is wired to a mainframe and a dedicated back-up system. There is even back-up power generation, because this is the lightening capital of the western world.

The front doors are made of bulletproof . . . not just shatterproof . . . glass. The three different types of Italian marble, seventeen brass and copper plaques, and two fountains confirm the amount of wasted taxpayer money. Guests must pass through two sets of metal detectors, and are then confronted by a black marble and cherry wood reception area run by three over-weight over-aged uniformed officers. For them, this is the last tour of duty before retirement. There are two lines of private citizens waiting for attention from the potentates of permission.

"My name is David Kermasic. I have an appointment with Officer Willow."

"Be seated. We'll call him."

The dozen or so hard-back plastic and chrome chairs and three complimentary faux-leather couches are filled with citizens. The table is littered with disorganized sections of the two local newspapers. I notice a door at the end of the lobby open and a young man, dressed in a blue shirt and khaki pants walks purposefully toward the assembled sitters.

"Mr. Kermasic?"

"Yes."

"Officer Anthony Willow. Please follow me."

We walk in silence the length of the lobby, through the door, down a corridor . . . two lefts, a right, and another left . . . to Interview Room 24-A.

"Please be seated. We appreciate you coming in today. We have just a few details, which we were hoping you could clarify. This won't take long. Would you like some coffee?"

"No thanks, I'm good."

"First, approximately how far from the automobiles and the victims were you when you took notice of them?"

"About 40 feet or so. I was parked, I think, five spaces and two rows from the two cars."

"When you heard the men talking, did you understand anything they were saying?"

"By the time I took notice of the men, they were yelling in Spanish. I don't speak Spanish. I did hear the words, motherfucker and cocksucker. Those were the only words I understood."

"How many shots did you hear?"

"I think I heard eight. There may have been more, but no less than eight."

"Describe what you were doing when you were hit by the bullet."

"I had stopped trying to enter my car and was about to walk over to the two parked cars to see about the guys. The shooting had stopped. Then one of the cars roared past me. It was being driven recklessly, weaving through the lane. It headed to the parking lot exit and shot down the street. Tires squealing. As I turned to the remaining car and the men, I was hit in the leg."

"Why would you walk over to the scene of a gun fight?"

"Well, I thought the shooting was over. I could see two men on the ground and assumed they had been hit. I thought I could be of some help if they were wounded."

"After you were shot, why did you continue toward the remaining car?"

"I thought at least one of them was alive. So I wanted to help him. I asked him not to shoot and called out that I wanted to help."

"Do you remember any details about the car that sped past you?"

"It was a dark four-door American car. I think GM. It was slung real low and had the wheels inverted. I believe the kids call them blades. The windows were tinted black. It had the new halogen headlamps and muted pink taillights. The car also had lights on the undercarriage."

"Do you remember the license number of the vehicle?"

"Yes, I gave the partial plate identification to the officers at the scene. The last three digits were L66. I think. These are the digits I recall. But, the car roared by so quickly, I could have mistaken the L for an I or a T or a J and the 6 for an 8 or a 5. But, I think it was L66. I can't remember anything about the first three digits. In fact, I'm not sure there were any. Maybe they were covered up or distorted somehow. I just don't know. Sorry."

"Nothing to be sorry about, Mr. Kermasic. We appreciate all the help you have been. And it's been a lot of help. Just a few more questions. When you got to the car could you tell if any of the men were alive?"

"I got to the two who were on the ground first. I don't know first aid, but I felt for a pulse on each of them. No pulses. Then I saw the two draped into the trunk. Again I looked for pulses. Nothing. That's when I went back to the office to report the shootings."

"Going back to the men on the ground. Did you notice that one of them had a crushed neck?"

"God, no. It's bad enough he was shot. Did someone break his neck?"

"Yes. We believe the either the driver of the car that almost hit you or a passenger in that car got out of the car and stepped on the victim's neck. Our ME reports that this victim died of a crushed trachea and the carotid artery in his neck . . . not the gunshot wounds. Our belief is that he would have lived if his neck had not been broken.

When you looked at the two men who had fallen into the trunk, did you see anything else in the trunk?"

"Just the trunk carpet and the pools of blood. Was there something there I didn't see?"

"Most likely not, sir."

"If I may ask. Why were those men killed? Why was the trunk open?"

"Mr. Kermasic, we believe the four men were killed in a drug deal that went bad. We further believe the occupant or occupants of the second car got out of the car after the shooting stopped, retrieved the drugs and perhaps cash from the trunk of the first car, and fled the crime scene with cocaine and cash. That is just where we are now. We have our sensors out in the community. We'll get the other bad guys. On behalf of the police department, I want to thank you for your cooperation. Most of all I want to express our appreciation of your bravery and caring for your fellow man. Please take my card. If you think of anything else, call me. Now let me show you out of this maze."

His smile was as plastic as the seats in the lobby. It's as if he knew that I knew that he knew I was a suspect. Was my replay of my crime scene testimony too exact? Inconsistent? Did I leave anything out? Did I add anything? Was I conned? Did he confirm his suspicions? What will his sensors report? How could I be shot, if both guys were already dead? How could the guy's neck be broken by some one in the departing car and the guy still shoot at me? This inconsistency must be explained away somehow. Who broke the guy's neck? Why? The fucker shot me? Revenge was a rush. Now, being a suspect is too. I can be involved, but on the edge of the big crime story. Sometimes scrambling for control is the jack. The fight is almost better than the victory. But, I must work hard to stay on the PD sonar screen as an innocent bystander.

IV

"Great list this week. What fish?"

The manager's pep talk.

"I wonder if we could cut to the chase and just ask them for their credit card before the pitch. No repetition. No heat. Just . . . *hey, I'm going to sell you a vacation package that you probably don't want, but with my skills and your stupidity, at the end of our conversation, you are going to give me your credit card so I can charge it with $599. So let's cut the shit and just give me the number now, so you can get on with your life and I can get to the next sucker. OK?* I bet that would work. Not always, but at least once."

"Yeah, Jimmy, that would be heaven. Come in here for an hour. Take six calls. Make three deals and go out and *pahtee*."

"Speaking' of *pahtee*, a little candy would taste nice."

"I indulged before I got here. But, I can always use some more now."

"I'm Jonesin'. Haven't scored in two weeks."

"Take the cigarettes. Go to the head. Just drop the pack off at my cube when you are done. Listen. Save me some. There is only enough for two hits. One for you. One for me. OK?"

"OK. If I like it, can I get more?"

"Tonight, no. But, if you like your taste, I can get some more Saturday. If you're interested, it's $80."

"I'll taste and tell you. I may be able to score for the guys in the house. Can you get a couple?"

"My man can get as much as I you can pay for in advance. Just let me know."

Dealing at the phone factory is so easy. This place is loaded with the lower strata of society. Ex-cons, junkies, and topless dancers populate the telehuckstering world. They didn't care about society before they got here and they don't care now. Jimmy drops my cigarette pack on my desk and gives me two thumbs up. I mouth *how much*. He'll let me know before by tomorrow's shift. Jimmy "Badger" Monteleone. The name reflects how he treats callers. He verbally abuses them until they either hang up or give it up. He is one of the more successful phone freaks in the room. No subtly in his performances. He has been warned about being abusive. But, he does get results. But, the room thrives on results. His exploits and successes are legendary. His Badger personality can also be seen outside the room, too. He can turn on friend and stranger alike without any apparent provocation. He's been in more bar fights that all of us put together.

The chatter from around the room indicates where the telehukster is in the process of closing.

"Of course you can take these vacations whenever you want during the year and you have three years to take them. Now, will you be using a Visa . . . ?"

"What exactly do you think your husband would not like about this gift?"

"You use a credit card for its protection. It's the safest way to buy anything. I believe your MasterCard starts with 5 . . ."

"Your young children will stay in your room. Now at these resorts your room is really a suite, because you are an award winner."

"Twelve days, a cruise, a car rental plus $400 worth of coupons for about one-fifth of the estimated retail price."

"We have to be on the up and up for American Express to let us use their services with their clients. American Express is the most difficult card to get and the most stringent system for a retailer to use. They are the best."

"The Florida Attorney General's office has personally visited us and approved of our business practices."

"If for some strange reason your Visa card can't hold the entire amount, we have the ability to split the bill to a second card."

"Discover card is issued by Sears. You know that this is the toughest card to get and for a retailer to use. Sears puts very tight restrictions on its card. We are honored to be among a select group of retail travel operations to be approved by Sears and Discover."

"It's your card, right? So you can use it as you want, right? You don't need your wife's approval to buy her a gift. Like at Christmas or her birthday. Get the material and take time with her to thoroughly review the vacations. Visa card numbers start with 4 . . ."

"Sun Shine Travel has been in business for nearly two decades and we are one of the nation's top five travel agencies. We could not have been in business that long and have been so successful if we failed to deliver on our promotions. I'm sure you agree that longevity is proof of success."

"We offer incredible savings as our promotion to get people to try our services. You'd agree that saving over $2,000 is a good idea, right. Would you like to save $2,000? I would."

"If you don't take advantage of this offer with this phone call, you'll never get another chance. I'd hate to see you miss out on the vacation opportunity of a life time."

"You'll get the package and can review it. Then you can decide when to take your vacations before the promotional fee shows up on your credit card bill. This means that you can make the final decision about the vacations with no real impact on your card account."

This is a great time to be a telemarketer. I have my weekly quota before the Friday shift. Poseidon has looked favorably upon me. Badger wants six grams. He'll have the money by the end of the shift. His roommate is dropping it off. I'll deliver after the Saturday shift. Then I'll head into the Combat Zone to see if I can sell a few more packets. Never the same bar two weeks in a row. Back to my favorite fishing hole.

*   *   *

Saturday is laundry and food shopping day. I start to look for a real place to live. Maybe a 2/2 for David and me. The paper is filled with ads showing beautiful young people splashing in the pool, playing tennis or golf, or just relaxing on the shoreline. These places are revolving doors. Too many singles. Too many drunks. Too much potential for police intervention. Need a place that is hidden, yet close to David's school. Off the beaten path, yet in an easy driving distance to everything. More mature population, yet not retirement age. A very, very, very middle class family community. I want to hide in plain sight. My budget is $700 per month. This search will take time. Ah, the joy of house hunting.

After shopping, I get on my cell phone and do my version of dialin' 'n smilin'. I am looking for a home; a new residence for David and me. A start for a better life. The options are few and far between. One house is on the eastside of the county. One in the next county to the west. I must take a look. Visits reveal the options are slim.

* * *

Saturday we catch the tail end of the list. The people the list broker added to fill his quota to Sun Shine. This group does not measure up. They are much smarter than those, who called during the week. These skeptics would question the ability of the sun to rise in the east. Few sales, but no *deeks*. This has been a good B week. My quota plus four. Two envelops next Friday. Delivery to Badger must be just between us . . . no roommates. Deal done. Off to shower, eat, and the Combat Zone. Prime time is 10-midnight.

The noise blaring from the open windows and doors of the clubs is meant to be an enticement. At my age, the cacophony is a repellant. But, I must be there, because that's where I can sell. The noise will be an umbrella under which I can conduct business. Eddie's Joint is packed. The under-30 crowd is gyrating spasmodically in front of five acne-faced greasy-haired skinny people, who apparently are responsible for the discordant composition. The bar is three deep. Eddie is one of the original entrepreneurs, who recognized the gold to be mined from this faux Bourbon Street.

I doubt if he has been to his Joint except to inspect the books and bribe the Fire Marshall. A Rolling Rock is to be nursed. Scan the crowd looking for a buyer. What the hell does a buyer look like? I don't have the foggiest idea. But, I start my probing. Get a dialog going with inanities for which I already have the right answers. Yelling some conversation over the dissonance and whispering the real words under it. I spy the Badger.

"Who's the band?"

"Beach Bashers. From Miami."

"Is it always this crowded?"

"Yeah. This is the best place. Best chicks. Easiest at least. Good music and no hassles. Bouncers all over the place. Any trouble and you're gone in a heartbeat. See that twosome at the end of the bar. The blondes. I've had my eye on them for fifteen minutes. Made good visual contact. Got a smile from both."

"So what does all that mean?"

"I'm going to buy them each a drink and see what happens."

"What could happen?"

"If they smile at me and give me a sign, I'll go over to them. I'll score with two chicks. Fanfuckingtastic."

"That's great. Hey, if someone wanted to make another kind of score, how could it happen?"

"Depends."

Now he is leaning into me. His eyes are glazed over. We are huddling. The first step of a deal. We whisper.

"Depends?"

"Yeah, it depends on what someone considers a score."

"Say, snow."

"Snow is available. One has to be very careful. I heard there are narcs all over the Zone and in the clubs. They claim to have snow, and then they entrap you. You give up your cash and your freedom for empty words. A bad trade."

Time to switch.

"I have access to a little, if you know anybody, who likes to ski."

"How much?"

The fish just clamped down on the hook, line and sinker.

"$80. And it's primo. Only can get two or three. Are you interested? It might be the icing on the cake for your two ladies."

"How do I know you're not a narc?"

"How do I know you're not one?"

"I'm not. Let me catch their reaction. I'll make my move and ask them if they are interested. If it's yes, I'll come back to you. If not, well that's life."

The two drinks arrive. The girls flash appreciative smiles and childlike flirting hand waves. They seem to be appreciative. Just how appreciative remains to be seen. I take the fish's seat as he casually strolls to the killing ground at the end of the bar. Another Rolling Rock. The din subsides. An ear-saving break. Almost imperceptibly, the bar crowd begins to thin. There are no covers or minimums at these clubs. So the herd thins with each set. The hard-core fans stay through the night.

"I'm back."

"I see."

"But I am empty handed for now. Those two are waiting for a few others . . ."

"Sorry about that."

Never display any emotion . . . fear, happiness, surprise, or anger. Always stay in control.

"I think I know someone who would like to go skiing."

"How often?"

"Well, this person would like to check out the base, before hitting the slopes big time."

"No problem. Where?"

"The person's car."

"Assuming I can acquire the snow, how often would this person like to ski?"

"She'll know after the test."

I look toward the two girls, who are now surrounded by four others. This could be the start of something big.

* * *

The girl's car is four blocks from the club. Parked in an alley. No streetlights or the ubiquitous video cameras on the lampposts like the main drag. There are two heads in the car. Both have long hair. The back door, passenger side, is opened as we arrive. I slide in and close the door before my bar connection can sit beside me. The two in the front seat never turn around. The thrill of the transaction is peaked by pseudo-secrecy. Like making love with a mask on. The deal broker paces woefully. Peering into the car, he so desperately wants to be part of the event. But, his part has been played.

"I understand from our mutual acquaintance that you two like to ski on good snow."

"True."

"I can access some fresh powder if you can afford it."

"$60, right?"

"Oh, too bad. Your guess was so close. Sorry, I can't find snow in that climate, at this time of year."

"$70?"

"You're very close, but no cigar. I have to leave now."

As I open the door, the driver turns. There is panic in her smile and voice. Her joy bringer is about to leave her and she will leave sad. Take away is the best way to sell.

"OK, $80, but we must taste test the merchandise first."

"How can I be sure you're not narcs?"

"How can we be sure that you're not one, too?"

"If I were a narc, you would not find out until after I leave the car."

"If we were narcs, you'd never leave the car. So, I guess none of us will know for sure until after the taste test. We are willing to risk it, if you have the balls."

The false bravado of a girl who is about to pee her pants is painfully obvious in the tenor of the voice. I reach into my inside shirt and withdraw a packet. I hand it to the passenger, who quickly inserts a rolled bill and snorts a huge hit. She passes the goodie bag to her friend, who repeats the insertion and nasal extraction. The packet is returned . . . much lighter.

"Good shit."

"Yeah, great stuff. Eighty percent pure. Thus, the price. I told your friend outside it was primo. I deliver on my promises. How much would you like?"

"Four."

"Yeah, four."

"I can do that here and now, if you have the bread."

"Count it. Six fifties and a twenty."

"Here is the merchandise. Nice doing business with you."

"If we want more, could you get more of this quality"?

"Yes, I can get more. How much would you like?"

"We don't know, yet?"

"When will you know?"

"Sometime this week. We'll call you."

"Not likely. You'll meet me."

"Where?"

"The Patio, next week at ten."

"Suppose we want a lot?"

"What do you consider a lot?"

"Fifteen. Twenty. Maybe thirty. Can you get that much?"

"I can get whatever quantity you need, if you can afford it. No credit. You buy with cash. You are free to do with what ever you want with what you buy. Strictly cash for candy. Is that clear?"

"Clear. Better count on us needing at least thirty. No make that fifty. Next week at The Patio at ten. Fifty. See you then."

She is so proud of herself. Playing the big game for the first time. Exiting the car and walking away was without event. When I got in the car I knew they were not narcs. They're university students, who are looking to deal the merchandise at $90 or $100. After a few deals, they'll figure out they can step on the coke and sell more than they bought. A real enterprise in the making. A conduit for me. Have to be wary they're not setting a trap at the push of the narcs. If I become overconfident, I'll get sloppy and get caught.

* * *

The week is slow. The list was bullshit and my attention is focussed on the next meeting. Why should

I suffer the slings and arrows of outraged callers just to make barely a living wage when I can make two months worth of telemarketing bullshit in ten minutes selling coke to college kids, who have more money than brains?

* * *

The Patio is just as noisy as Eddies. The crowd looks the same. Even the bartenders and bouncers look like clones. Wouldn't be a kick if there were only one set of people . . . drinkers, bartenders, and bouncers. And this single set moved from club to club with each break the band took. The breaks were staggered and lasted 45 minutes so that each club could prosper. A moveable party. Weird.

Arriving at 10:30, I take a position at the back of the bar facing the door. In about ten minutes, a young woman settles in beside me.

"Ya know, I'd rather be skiing in South America. Have you ever skied the Andes Mountains? The snow is so pure it takes your breath away. It's damned near orgasmic."

"How many times have you skied the Andes?

"Fifty times."

Now we huddle as if we're getting intimate.

"Do you have the money with you?"

"It's in the car."

With that she kisses my earlobe.

"Go to your car. Get the money and come back here. Then we will go to my car for the snow."

I lick her ear.

"I'm not sure that's a good idea."

She licks me.

"To ease your worries, I'll walk with you to the car."

I touch my tongue to her neck. The small hairs respond.

"Then what?"

She insinuates her tongue, filling my ear.

"Then we go to my car and you get the candy, little girl."

I drag my tongue from her clavicle to ear. No wetness just sensual pressure. I see the dew in her eyes. She likes what is happening. Foreplay in public drives most women wild. An open display of the most personal nature. Very forbidden. Very Victorian. She breaks the huddle and knocks back her drink.

"Walk with me. Not behind."

We walk down the side of the clubs, across three streets, and left into the same alley. I like the cane. I really don't need it, but it's a cool affectation. All the while we walk; she holds my arm and rubs her bra-less upper torso on me. If this is an act, it is good. If it is for real, I know what to do about it.

"Here we are."

"Get the money from the car and come with me to my car."

She doesn't hesitate. Opens the door, reaches under the front seat, and removes a manila envelope.

"Leave your purse in the car. Just take your keys."

Not a word. She is cool.

We walk the five blocks to my car. The clutching and rubbing continues. At one intersection she kisses me tenderly. A submissive, seductive kiss. She gets in the passenger side of the car. I lock the doors and windows. We head off into the night. Is she on tranqs? Not one iota of anxiety. No usual questions or idle chatter.

"You don't trust me do you?"

"In my line of sales, I trust no one. The first deal went smoothly, but this is major weight. I have no idea who you are? So trust is at a premium."

"I don't know who you are either. I'm here on faith. A real risk for a real reward. I have what you need. I have a distribution system. A wealthy and hungry distribution system. It's mine and not yours. You have what I need. You have the product to distribute through my system. It's yours and not mine. We need each other. If my clients are happy with your product, we both can make money. We form a partnership. A business arrangement. Anything beyond that is a mistake. But, a physical relationship must never interfere with our business partnership. It's all about the money. That's why I'm here. Those are my rules."

The physical overtures were part of her game. Testing the waters. Am I a business partner or just some dealer looking to get laid? She is convinced I am the former. I passed the test. We pull into a large shopping mall parking lot.

"The stuff is in the cavity of the pull-down arm rest in the back seat. Check it out."

She exits and re-enters the car. Finds the brown bag and counts the packets. She doesn't trust me entirely.

"All here. Count your money."

Twenty $100's and forty $50's. Cash is a good thing. She is back in the front seat.

"If you can handle it, I can move at least fifty a week for sure. Maybe more. You and I should plan to meet and consummate . . . oops bad word . . . complete our transaction every Friday or Saturday. I need to be able to reach you during the week, if there is a snag in my plans."

"The deal is fine. The reaching out to me is not fine. Each week when you make the buy, we'll decide where and when we will meet the next week. I will be there. If I am not there, something catastrophic has happened. I will assume the same for you. If we do not meet, our next connection will be at the last rendezvous spot. Do you understand?"

"Yes, that's fine. Total anonymity. It excites me."

"It's insurance. It's just the way it is. Now let me take you back to your car."

No talking during the trip back to the Zone. Silence. Real partners don't have to make noise. They know what the other is thinking. At the drop off, we agree on fifty. Next Saturday night at Leapin' Lizards at 10:30. On my way home I notice that more and more cars have those ultra-bright halogen headlights, and that undercarriage lighting . . . green, red, and blue . . . is visible on nearly one in five cars. When did all this happen? Where was I?

* * *

Another week of a shit list. Thank God for my burgeoning enterprise. I have to be careful not to use my own product. The business is primary. Pleasure derived from my goods is to be experienced by those who pay for the packets. Not the seller. Badger wants eight more on Friday, but can't have the money until Saturday. No deal. He begs. There is a threatening tone in his voice. I take away his pleasure. He wants it more. The next day he says he will have the money for me at the end of Thursday's shift. I will deliver on Friday. He now understands the rules of business.

Friday is Jack Night. One of the women, Jackie, who works the nightshift used to be a topless dancer. She hooked patrons in one of the backrooms. The court ordered her to change employment or lose her child. She supplements her present telemarketing income by hooking on Friday. Just the people in the office. Guys and gals. Her car is her secondary place of employment. Rumor is that she likes what she does. No one has ever been disappointed. I pass. I must concentrate on my real job. It's all about the money.

* * *

Sunday with David is too damned short. And it's becoming almost sterile. I pick him up. We do stuff. We eat at restaurants. I have no home where we can just hang out. Watch sports on TV or rent actions movies for the VCR. I have to get a place. Move that up to #1 on my list of must do.

David notes that I seem to have trimmed down over that last few weeks. Tell him, I can't stop the aging process, but I don't have to be old and fat. Work has been tough. I need extra time to get the callers to give up their credit cards. They are very skeptical. Takes the full hour to get my quota of six. No time for breaks or the evening meal. I am too tired and it's too late to eat after the shift. Worked a double or two each week. Twelve hours of repeating the same pitch. Twelve hours of repetitive pressure to sell, sell, sell. After these days, sleep is instantaneous and deep. Hunger satiating must wait until breakfast.

* * *

In my room I pour over the Real Estate Sections of both papers. David has told me he hates living in a 2/1 college dorm complex. I look for houses to rent. None that I can afford in the neighborhoods he likes. Make a list of six within my price range . . . all in or near the farm sections of the counties. Driving to and fro, but seclusion. Check them out Monday. Go to the office and use the outbound lines. Found a good choice. Maybe not ideal. It's far from everything. Farmhouse with no fancy build outs or amenities. Just basic living. Sits on an acre. Part of a 95-citrus grove. Land owned by someone up north. Revenue derived from rental and orange crop. Grove worked by neighbor. Price is a little over my budget, but the setting is ideal. They will get back to me after the credit check. That will show me as a big risk. I'll write whatever sized check it takes to get the place. I've got the money now.

* * *

The list of losers continues. Most thought the vacations were free and that they had won them. They aren't keen enough to know they were conned into calling. A sample certificate sits at every body's cube. It looks like a stock certificate. It is masterfully written and laid out. The clear impression is that the recipient has won the free vacations. Upon close inspection of the opening sentence, the caller can realize that he or she has been awarded two things: a free phone call and the right to buy the vacations.

There is so much gobbledygook and quasi-legal looking text on both the front and back of the certificate that any recipient would be confused. Not sure how this was approved by the State Attorney General's office. Maybe it wasn't. If it wasn't, it will have to be revised once the regulators see it. That's the lifestyle of the flimflam industry. Stay one step ahead of the regulators and fight every required modification to business practices. Delay and partial compliance are the rules for this industry.

The results for the day shift suck. At night, we can expect no better. I had no luck at all. My first blank in over six months. Not since I left days. I couldn't care less. Not to panic. Rachel, who goes by the names, Bobbi Bettmann, Sally Preacher, Jane Wilson, and Lisa Martin, has been put on probation for failing to meet quota two weeks in a row. Hell, only a few have met quota during the weeks of the shit list. But, management must enforce its rules to keep the rest of us in line. So she is the sacrificial lamb. She will undergo training, counseling, and monitoring.

All the while working the shit list and becoming more and more frustrated and desperate. She can't panic and sell heat just to make a deal. She must stay with in the prescribed, tried and true guidelines. These are the guidelines that the regulators have begrudgingly sanctioned. Using them and not heat keeps the company off the regulatory sonar screen. The company punishes the telemarketers for doing what the company tells us to do. All just to protect its own financial ass. We are fucking pawns. If all goes per usual, Rachel will be gone in two weeks. She'll be replaced by some naïve housewife, who may or may not last six months.

The average life span in these rooms is nine months. I am a dinosaur. People stay until they are discovered or until they hear of a room offering a little bit more or better lists or an easier sell. Some bogus promise gets the hucksters to move. These people have known each other for years. Different rooms. Same faces. They settle. Shift. Reshuffle the room mix. Meet again. Start the process again. War stories. Horror stories. Music played so loudly that the huckster has to yell. Anything to push enthusiasm. Make the deal. A bell is rung and the huckster's name is posted with each deal. So that everybody knows they are in a race.

Low pay per deal, but nice bonuses. Forty dollars a deal. Three deals a day for two days earns $100 in cash. Lots of money paid in cash. Off the books pay is the rule not the exception. Less expensive for the company. More money for the huckster. But, some money must show up as income to keep the company an employee off the federal sonar screen. Success stories posted on the board are ostensibly carrots. Really, the success stories are cudgels. It's always interesting that day success stories are posted for the night shift and vice versa. We can never verify the accuracy of the numbers. Most of the posted information is a lie to encourage or embarrass. The nights drag on. Is it the list, the job or anticipation about Saturday night?

* * *

Leapin' Lizards is not quite jammed. The band is on break and the revelers have begun to change venues. From my perch at the end of the bar I spot her. Her entrance is that of a queen. She is a *smokin' hottie*. Light blue chambray, lose-fitting-midriff-exposing top and bright white hip huggers. Her stomach is flat with just enough flesh on the exterior for sensuality.

She strides in on red Fuck Me ankle-wrapped, three-and-one-half-inch-heels. Gold coin earrings, gold coin dangling from the single strand necklace, three gold bracelets, and two gold rings. Fendi bag over her shoulder. No bra. No need. Her breasts appear to be so firm as to not jiggle. Can't see a panty line or even a thong line. Most male and some female eyes are on her. She glides through the Hormone Sea to me. A gentle kiss on my lips is all for show and none for go.

"Grey Goose. Double. One rock. How have you been?"

"Terrific. Were I any better, I'd have to be twins. And you, partner?"

"All is very well. Business is better than I thought it would be. There is a big demand across the land. People clamoring for joy and salvation. Money in their hands, they approach the citadel of commerce. Calling for your product. Shall we consummate . . . oops there's that bad word again."

"Join me in my chariot."

As we leave the crestfallen males smile painfully at my apparent success. Their dates scowl. We walk, hand in hand to my car. I have discarded the cane. For six blocks she leans her torso against me at every opportunity. I like it as much as she does. We drive to a spot beneath the interstate. A truck parking lot in the midst of a community of homeless. Actually, this is their home. So they're not truly homeless.

"This time money first."

"How much did you bring?"

"Five large, like we agreed."

"Damn."

"What?"

"I could use sixty. That's why I want to be able to reach you during the week. People, who would not normally be customers, sampled your product and loved it. Demand happened. I need the supply."

"We do not talk during the week. Anonymity, remember. It's my never-to-be-broken rule. Besides, those who don't receive will have a greater desire next week.

Get some of the buyers to share with others. Build your customer base. Build your business. But, to be successful, you must control the distribution of product. Stay in control. Lose control and you lose your business. Now the money."

We exchange packages. Hundreds and fifties. It's all there. She is satisfied.

"Now what?"

"Now, sweetheart, I take you back to the Zone or your car and we go our separate ways."

"Before we do all that. I want you to know that this partnership is the most exciting thing I've ever done. I make money and I have enough product for my own recreation."

The alarm went off in my head.

"If you choose to use the stuff, you choose to lose. If you lose control, I am in jeopardy. I don't like jeopardy, not even the TV game. If you use, you will make a serious error in judgment. And that error could be costly to you and me. Be very, very careful. The stuff is like tapeworm. It creates, in its host, the feeling of invincibility, while the worm lives off the fiber of the host. The host is conned into thinking it's in control. It can feed the worm or not as the host decides. But, the reality is that the worm's in control. You must feed the worm or die. You have no choice. Your highs become less high and don't last very long. The worm wants more and more and more. Each week. Each day. You'll reach a point where one gram is not enough to get you going in the morning . . . ."

"Stop the pedantic medical and psychological claptrap. If I didn't use recreationally, I would have never met you. If I never met you, I wouldn't be in business now. So, be positive. Don't be the voice of doom and gloom. Think success. Yours, mine, and ours. Now the big question. Do you want a taste?"

"No! I don't use when I sell."

"I mean a taste of me. I know we said no touching. But, I'm in the mood for you. Here and now."

"The answer is the same. No. Business and pleasure are a lethal combination."

"OK, I'll charge you. What ever you want for $100. And I mean what ever you want. What ever you can dream a woman can do for you, you can have with me now for $100. A good business offer."

"Thanks, but no thanks."

* * *

The ride back to her car is sullenly silent. I head for home. I pull into the drive and park behind the eight year old rusted four-door that belongs to my landlords. Or vice versa. Lock my car. Notice a sedan with parking lights creeping along the street.

"Excuse me, sir. Could you help us?"

I never leave my spot beside my car. The sedan is less than twenty feet from me now. The speaker does not lean out of the window, but his countenance is lit by the car's interior lights. I see a man with shoulder length hair and a long flowing moustache. He has a round silver stud in his right ear.

"Sure. If I can."

"We're looking for a gentleman named Jerry Kermasic. We know he lives around here somewhere. Do you know where he lives?"

"Sorry, I can't be much help. I'm just in town visiting my grandparents. Just here for the week. I don't know any of the neighbors."

"You see, sir, Mr. Kermasic has something which belongs to us. He called us tonight and told us he would like to return it. So we drove here to get it from him."

"As I said, I don't know any of the neighbors. So, I wouldn't be able to help you find this Mr. Kermasic."

"Sir, maybe you could ask your grandparents if they know Mr. Kermasic. We would be obliged."

"They're sleeping. I don't want to wake them. I'm sure you understand."

"Yes we do. Thanks for your time, sir. Goodnight."

I turn to enter the house through the back door. The sedan backs out of sight. Never revealing the license plate. Cold sweat and nearly audible palpitations accompany me to my room. I can't sleep.

V

The call to officer Willow goes to his voice mail. How the hell did they find me?

David has gone out of town with some school buddies for the weekend, so I am alone with my anxiety . . . my panic. But, I am excited. Fear is a rush. Breakfast and a few Bloody Marys will fuel the fire. My pager interrupts a reading of the Sports Section, I go to the pay phone.

"Mr. Kermasic. This is Officer Willow returning your call. How can I help you?"

"Officer Willow, I'm scared. Last night as I was coming home, some guys pulled up to my house and asked me if I knew where Jerry Kermasic lived. No one in that neighborhood knows my name. Not even the people from whom I rent. I have no lease and I pay in cash. The car these guys were driving was a dark sedan with colored undercarriage running lights and blacked-out windows. When they were done with their questioning, they backed away so I couldn't see the license plate.

I'm sure it was the car from the murders and drug deal. YA' know the car that almost hit me and got away. They know where I live. No one knew I was a witness to the murders. No one except the police. So, I have to figure that someone in your department told the thugs who I was and where I lived. The thugs came by to frighten me. They were successful. Now I need protection. Protection from the same police department that told these thugs about me."

"Take it easy, Mr. Kermasic. Try to relax. I need you to come down to the station and make a statement so we can take appropriate action to help you."

"That would be the dumbest thing imaginable. I come down to the station. I am seen. Seen by the guy or guys who leaked my name to the killers and drug dealers. These cops let the dealers know that I reacted to their threat of last night. They then have me locked in their sights. They know I am the witness. That I can testify against them. Next week these guys come by my house again, scoop me up, and take me to a deserted field where I become a permanent part of the landscape. A feeding farm for ants and rats. No thanks, Officer Willow, I won't be coming down to the station."

"Then we'll meet somewhere. I'll take your statement. You can sign it. Then we can give you protection. Where are you now? Where would you like to meet?"

"The zoo at 1:30. By the big cats' cages. See you there."

Is Willow the informant? For whom does he really work? I am afraid. Very afraid. But living on the edge of safety and danger is a jack. I crave the jack. It is my drug of choice.

* * *

There's something almost hypnotic about the big cats. Their stride is fluid. And when they are stretched out they seem to melt into the surface on which they are resting. Willow waits for me.

"I'm going to record our meeting today while I write it down. When we're through, you can sign the statement."

"I'll need a copy of the statement."

"No problem, there's a Qwik-Copy Center down the street. The city will even pay for the copy."

"Before we begin, I want you to know that although I am here today with you and that I'm about to give a statement about last night, I'm not absolutely *posifuckingtively* sure you are 100% clean. By that I mean I am concerned there is a leak from your department to the thugs. Why not you? You could be the leak. You have free access to the reports and records. You have primary knowledge of what happened that night. Who and what the police think caused the murders. You have the files. You could be the leak. What's to say you're not?"

"If you would be comfortable giving your statement to another officer or even my Lieutenant, this can be arranged."

"Then it goes into the same files. Your files."

"I'm fucked if I do and fucked if I don't. Heads I lose. Tails you win."

"Mr. Kermasic, I understand your concern. We, at the department, have our suspicions that there is some connection between certain members of the police department and organized crime. A connection that goes deeper than just guys who grew up in the old neighborhood and went different ways. Some went to JC and the Academy. Some dropped out of high school and made a living from the streets. I can't go into any more detail, but we are aware of several cases that have been compromised. We are looking to clean our own house, so to speak. All I can do is assure you that the information you give me will be held in the strictest confidence and that I will personally supervise your protection."

"Your assurance aside, I am going on faith here. And my faith in a confessed dirty police department is not particularly strong."

"How about having faith in a police officer, who hopes to make a career move from these crimes? An officer, who stands to get a two-grade promotion and a bunch of commendations when he solves the crime. Put your faith in me. Put your faith in my greed and aspirations. And, I'll protect the only witness I have. You. 100% faith and 100% protection. Me and you. OK?"

"Fair enough. I can trust someone who exposes his own agenda."

I repeat the events and conversation of last night leaving out the incriminating details.

"Mr. Kermasic, I will arrange for you to have 24/7 protection. I'll have an unmarked car follow you during the day and tuck you in at night. I'll even ride along whenever I can, which will be often. All I ask is that you call me and let me know of your driving plans. I'll notify the officer in the car. He will be with you. Fore knowledge helps us keep a clear eye on you. It's for your protection. Do we have a deal?"

"Done deal."

On my way to the beach for an afternoon of nap, I stop by the branch Post Office I have used as a legal address since the divorce. I stop by once a week. That's often enough to pick up the bills, flyers, and blind solicitations. Soon I'll have no bills and a real address. So I can get totally different solicitations. The wad of mail is jammed into P.O. Box 45050. I stand at the table and sort. Keep. Trash. Keep. Trash. Trash. A hand addressed letter. Looks like a woman's hand. Post marked Dothan, Alabama.

> *Dear Jerry,*
>
> *We had so much fun the last time we were with you. We owe you something. We will be in Tampa the weekend of the 11-14 staying at the same Holiday Inn. We'd really, really, really like to see you on Saturday night. You are the best. If you want to see us, call and ask for Tina Johnston, room 314.*
>
> *Please,*
> *Tina and Dottie*

My double header wants an encore. The gods have a way of balancing a mortal's life. How did they get my address? My wallet. The vixens lifted my wallet that night in the motel. They copied down my name and address. My P.O . . . not where I sleep. I'll call on Thursday and leave a message. See them after my regular deal in the Zone. Nothing can interfere with business. Not even my pleasure.

Tampa Ledger May 8, 2013
Two Bobbers

At approximately 8:30 PM Sunday, a pleasure boat, returning to harbor ran afoul of the bodies of two men in Harbor Side Channel. The victims' arms and legs were bound. The neck of each victim had been twisted and broken so that the victim was facing backward. Additionally, the all ten fingers had been severed. The victims' identities are unknown at this time although they are reputed to be members of the street gang, "Nieve Lobo". Nieve Lobos (Snow Wolves) derives it name from the drug the gang deals . . . cocaine. The killings appear to represent escalation in the gang wars, which have plagued the city for over two years. The official police spokesman will neither confirm nor deny any connection between these latest murders and the brutal shootings on the city's westside four weeks ago.

However, an anonymous source close to the Organized Crime Task Force has stated that these killings could be retaliation for the murders. There is suspicion among the task force that the westside murders were the result of a drug deal gone bad. When the police arrived the drugs and cash were missing. Speculation is that there were others at the original crime scene and that they fled with the cocaine and money. The two floating bodies are suspected of being two opportunistic thieves from the westside shoot out. Their necks were twisted as a demonstration of how they had turned against the gang. Their fingers were cut off to show they had taken something that did not belong to them.

The full brunt of the police force has been rededicated to solving these two separate, but seemingly related crimes, and putting an end to the violence the has made this city the crime capital of the Southeast.

* * *

I let Willow know that I will be home, food shopping and then going to work from 4 to 10. Three packets in my wash. If they were full, I lost money. If they were empty before the laundry, I'm using too much of my own product. Lose. Lose. The murder story is the buzz and source of all speculation among the barely educated of the night shift. Little attention is paid to the day shift's lack of success as displayed on the board: 11 deals, 16 *deeks.* The list from hell continues. And the pressure to sell increases exponentially. It now borders on intimidation and insults.

"Well ma'am if you have no interest in the vacations, why did you call?"

"Is that you can't afford the $599, or that you can't make a decision on your own?"

"This can't be too much money for someone in your position."

"This award is good for a very limited time. If you decide not to take advantage of our promotion with this phone call, and if you hang up without securing the vacations, we will give the award to the next person who calls and has a valid certificate. You wouldn't want to make a foolish mistake like that now would you?"

"I can tell you're an intelligent consumer, who uses his credit card often. You know that you can buy an article of clothing, take it home, show your husband, and return it if the two of you think it is not right. The purchase amount never shows up on your credit card statement, because you received a balancing credit before the end of the billing cycle. It's the same with these vacations."

"Could you explain to me why you would fail to take advantage of a $2,500 savings? I'm sure you take advantage of savings everyday. These vacations are just like those other savings."

"If it was me, I'd secure the vacations, review the materials with my wife, and then make a fully informed decision. I would not pass up this tremendous opportunity and have to explain my lack of self confidence to my wife."

"Nowhere on the certificate does it say that the vacations are free. But, you can secure ten nights at Disney World, the Bahamas, and Cancun and save over $2,500. If you're interested in great vacations and saving money, we should talk. If you're not interested in great vacations, and not interested in saving $2,500, you should hang up now."

"I'm confused. Help me understand why you would not take advantage of this incredible offer. You do take vacations, right? And, you do like to save a lot of money, right. And, you'd like to go to the Caribbean. Mexico, and Disney, right?"

"Sir, the Florida Department of Commerce, which regulates all business in the state, has given Sun Shine the highest rating in customer satisfaction. Sun Shine Travel has been in business for nearly two decades. I'm sure you'll agree that you can trust the regulators and our heritage of success. You can rely on this offer."

The pushing and goading goes on and on. Four hours and I have one, very shaky deal and two *deeks*. Badger has two deals. He claims they are rock solid. When the going gets tough, Badger gets the card.

"Jerry, YA know what I think."

"Yeah the list shits."

"Nah, about the two bobbers in the channel. I think the cops and the media are wrong. The two guys were not killed in retaliation for taking the candy and the cash. They were killed because they failed to protect the merchandise. They failed to do what they were hired to do. I bet they were muscle at the crime scene. The deal went sour, and these assholes ran for their lives. They left the goods at the scene and ran like cowards. And somebody else took the goodies. Lobos Nieve is a vicious street gang. I hear they're part of "YA". "YA" is how the Spanish pronounce double "L". And double "L" stands for Loco Lobos."

Loco Lobos is a new type of gang. No territories, just specialties. "YA" oversees the activities of various packs each centered on one type of crime. They have packs for every type of crime. There's the pack that deals with gambling . . . Lobos Bolitos. There's the gang that deals with extortion and loan sharking . . . Lobos Dineros. And these guys, Lobos Nieve. They are strictly into drugs. Each pack reports to an Alpha Male. The Alpha Males form a commission, which runs the entire operation.

Loco Lobos, I heard, is trying to take over the westside. Take over the hookers, drugs, and gambling. They finance their way into the westside by dealing. They always send protection for the big deals. This time the protection failed. The guys that ran had to pay the price for failure. So, "YA" sends an obvious message to whoever really took the merchandise. And here is the best part. The people, who actually took the goodies, see what "YA" does to its own and run scared. They can't return the merchandise, unless they leave it under a tree and tell YA where it's at. So, they have to just disappear. Leave the area. Ah, the power of advertising."

"That's very interesting, Badger. But, too convoluted. Why wouldn't "YA" put pressure on the guys who ran from the deal to find the merchandise? Why would they kill two of their own?"

"Because the can. And because getting the drugs back is more important than a couple of foot soldiers. They want to send a message to everyone. Don't fuck with "YA".

"On that happy note, let's get back to our stations."

"Jerry, I'm curious. Has anybody approached you about what you saw that night?"

"No one outside of the police and this office knows I was at the crime scene when the shooting and robbery occurred. How would a stranger contact me unless they got information from the cops or someone here? Besides I don't talk to strangers. My mother taught me well. I told the police everything. I was shot. Nearly run over by an unknown assailant. Walked to the car. Found the bodies and the empty trunk. Came to this office and called 911. The guys in the car that nearly ran me over, must have crushed the victim's neck, emptied the trunk, and fled. I think the cops are right. Let me ask you, Badger. How do you know so much about "YA"?"

"Native intelligence, my man. I grew up in the same neighborhood that most of these guys did. I know their names."

The week moves at a snail's pace. The hucksters desperately trying to separate the callers from their wallets, while the callers guard their money like Rotweilers. Wednesday, the rental agent calls to tell me the place is mine. Mine if I can come up with the first and last month's rent plus a month's security by tomorrow. A check for $2,550 and the place is mine for the year. My credit rating was not good. I have the cash. Thursday night it is raining heavily. It wasn't raining when I came to work, so my car is parked six rows from the building. I think I spot the surveillance car. It's parked in the far corner of the lot. I need to pick up candy for my Saturday sale. Ask Badger if I can borrow his car to run a half-hour errand

"Don't get into no accidents, man, or I'll kill yer ass."

Somehow, I believe him. The surveillance car does not see me get into Badger's car and leave the parking lot. So, it can't follow me. I'm back with my booty, before Badger can get edgier that he normally is. I wear the bag with the hundred + packets under my shirt. Friday is an A payday. A low point in my revenue stream.

* * *

Saturday is a special son and dad day. We drive to the country to see our new home. He has to keep his eyes closed as we get near. I am more excited than he is. Finally, as we bounce down the drive, he cheats.

"Is this your new place, dad?"

"David this is *our* new place. Three bedrooms. Two baths. Eat-in kitchen, separate dining room and living room. Big back porch. And a ton of land. Plus, we're about a half-mile from a lake, so we can fish. Maybe even catch and eat. Won't that be a kick? The best part is that now you can stay with me over night. Even for weekends. All I have to do is get the court to agree that this is a safe and suitable place for you to stay and live, and we can be a just a couple of guys. I can take you to school from here. Wait'll you get a look inside."

His eyes smile. I sense a weight lifted from his shoulders. As we approach the house a pick up comes beside us.

"Hey, Mr. Kermasic. Is this David? David, I'm Bob Potter. Boy, you really look like your dad. I wonder if all sons look like their dads. My boy does too, so they say. I work the land around your house. My place is over there past the grove. You can't see it. At night you can see the lights from my place and now I'll be able to see the lights from yours. David, your dad told me you like to fish. The lake is well stocked. The name of the lake is Lac Baton. That's Stick Lake.

Named after the mangroves that cover the shore. Named by the French Doctor, who left Napoleon and sailed to the New World. He discovered Safety Harbor. His name was Philippe something. When you want to fish, just walk down the path over there to the dock. My boat is pulled up on the shore. We can all go out to the middle of the lake and catch the big ones. You can fish from the dock or the boat, but not the shore.

There are Gators in the lake. At least two big ones on the far side. I suspect a male and female. People can't swim in the lake. The lake belongs to the Gators. They just let us take some fish from in once and a while. Got to be careful. Don't feed or tease the Gators. And, don't go near them during the mating season. The male takes that as a real threat. My son will tell you. A while back a stray dog wandered to the shore. My boy, he's twelve, saw the whole thing. The big Gator got the dog and dragged it under the water to the place where the Gator saves food. So, you have to be careful. My boy's name is Bob, too. Goes to Palm Middle School. Loves to fish. Fishes more than does his studies. Hey am I talking too much. Just glad to have neighbors, I guess. Well I'll leave you two to check out your new place. Call me if you need anything."

He roars out the drive. I wonder if he will see my tag-along cop.

"Dad, did he breath during that monologue? That guy seems starved for company. I wonder if there is there a Mrs. Potter"

"Don't know. Maybe he's just glad to see another man. I do know that my job is to get the household up and running. Come on let's check out our new digs."

We walk through the house, inspecting each room. Small talk about where furniture will go. With each room David seems happier. His face reflects the optimism about our future. He will make contributions to this new life we build. This is the same feeling enjoyed by a husband and wife in the first home. I remember vaguely from years ago.

"I brought a cooler with sandwiches and some sodas. Our first meal in our new house. After lunch, we'll walk down to the dock. Later we'll go to a furniture store to check out stuff for our bedrooms and the living room. I won't bore you with the stuff for the kitchen. I'm going as fast as I can. The sooner the court approves this, the sooner we can be together."

"I don't mean to be nosy. But, how can you afford all this. I mean from a furnished room to a house to be furnished."

"I have worked hard and denied myself a lot. Saved enough money over the past year to take this big step. Two things, though. We can't buy all the furniture at once. We'll sparsely furnish each bedroom first. Then the living room. Last will be the dining room. In four or six months the house will be furnished like it is really ours. Second, I'm going to try this on my own. No roommate other than you. But, if I think things are getting too tight, I'll have to get a roommate. Maybe one of the guys from work. And, I'll do it quickly so I don't fall back into the pit of debt. So far I've been able to make all the deposits and down payments. The deposits were more than I had suspected because of my bad credit. I just have to push hard at work to have the money for us to live. We've made it this far. Only a little farther. Let's see this dock."

The day is great. David examines prices on every piece of furniture. He keeps a budget in his journal. The journal from school is for the kids to record their days and then to write about their experiences as a traveler's diary. This day will make great fodder for his term paper. A light meal and then drop him at his mother's. The deal is he can't mention anything of the new place to her. I will do this via the court system. This will be tough for him, but he swears he can do it.

* * *

I notify Willow that I'm going to the Combat Zone for a night of drinking. The surveillance car will baby sit my car. No place to sit at the bar. I find a table near the door to await my distributor. Around 10:45, in she saunters dressed like an urban cowgirl wannabe. Jeans, a brocade long-sleeved denim shirt, and expensive three-leather boots make up her costume. The silver and gem encrusted belt buckle is the highlight and only accent. Her smile has none of the anticipated coquettish charm, lure of the seductress, or the warmth of a business friend. It exhibits pain and fear.

"I need a double Gray Goose. Neat."

In two long sips the hammer is dropped. No hello. No flirtation. Just belt and bolt. We are out the door too fast.

"I've got the cash. Let's go to your car do the deal and let me get on my way."

"Tonight we'll take your car. But, I'll drive. Keys please. I don't mean to be presumptuous, but there appears to be something wrong. You seem distracted or something."

"Nothing's wrong. I just want to get this nonsense over with and back to my paying customers."

On our way to the parking lot behind the Sanitation Department, I make more lefts and rights than an Albanian taxi driver. I even double back on my course. If there is a tail on us, it is lost. She is very nervous. I notice she is wearing a bra. Not like her. The long-sleeved shirt buttoned to the top is also not like her. The full blousing of the shirt is really not like her. She is fidgeting. She picks up her purse twice. It's not her regular Fendi, but a big black bag. I notice her eyes. Dark circles around them and they appear to be slightly sunken. Has she been crying? Has she used too much of the product? Something is out of synch.

"Are you sure you're OK? Are you sick or not feeling well? You just don't seem to be yourself tonight."

"I'm fine. Just tired. Now can we do the deal? I've got the cash. Do you have the coke?"

She has never used those words before.

"Come here."

I take her in my arms and kiss her deeply. My tongue explores her mouth and her oral snake reciprocates. She clutches and I begin groping. I cup her right breast through the blouse and bra. Massage to stimulate. Then I unsnap the second and third snaps to get to her bra. She pushes me away.

"I thought we agreed. No physical stuff. Just business."

"I couldn't resist. You're so sexy tonight."

There it is. The light kicks off the minute piece of metal. The pin microphone stuck in her bra. The bitch is wired. I hold her close and whisper.

"Who got to you? The cops?"

She begins to cry. No sobbing just tears pouring down each side of her nose. She scrambles through her purse and retrieves a pen and small note pad.

Customer told police about me. Arrested Monday. If I get recording of our deal, I go free. Wire planted this evening. What could I do?

I write.

No tape tonight. No merchandise. No deal. Show them money. Tell them we meet next Saturday. Same place and time. I'll think of something by then. It's OK. You'll be safe.

There's less pain in her smile. Return to the Zone in silence. She drives off never to see me again. Let her explain that to the cops. It's her weight. She wanted to play and now she must pay. Time for my double header.

* * *

Park near room 314. Exiting the car, I hear a car stopping between the motel and me. I turn and out of the corner of my eye I glimpse something swinging at my leg. The noise, *tunk*, precedes the excruciating pain above the knee, directly on the bullet wound. A crowbar can cause pain so intense that it muffles sound. I am on the parking lot surface just trying to stay conscious. I vaguely hear the voices demanding that I return what is theirs and not mine. If I don't return their merchandise and their money, they will fix it so that there is no joy at all in my life. I see an arm raised. The hand clutches the long black rod. The swing is straight down. The second hit is near the first. Training and perseverance allow for such accuracy. As I begin to pass out from the pain, I see twinkling red, white and blue stars. So do my assailants. They book. Moments later, I sneeze from the inhalant cracked under my nose.

"Mr. Kermasic, are you OK?"

My guardian angels in blue. Actually, one angel is wearing a light colored shirt and khaki pants. I sense

Officer Willow's outline. The window curtains in room 314 draw closed. The lights are turned off. I quit. The next time I can focus on anybody, I am on a gurney in St. Joseph's ER.

VI

"Mr. Kermasic, did you recognize the men who attacked you?"

"No sir."

"Do you know any reason you should be attacked?"

"No sir"

"What were you doing in the parking lot of the Holiday Inn at the time of the attack?"

"I was there to visit a friend."

"What's your friend's name?"

"That's irrelevant. Am I a suspect or a victim?"

"Sir, we have to explore every possibility dealing with the attack. One possibility is that your attackers were somehow connected with the friend you were going to visit."

"Officer, I'll take over for now. Could you leave us alone?"

A friendly face.

"Officer Willow, when can I get out of here?"

"The doctor said the X-rays are negative. No break, but a massive bone bruise and deep contusion. Some shredding of the thigh muscle. You'll need a tight leg wrap and a lightweight cast for about four weeks. The kind you can take off for bathing and replace later. The purpose of the cast is to constrain the thigh so it can heal faster and with no long-term disfigurement. You'll have limited mobility, but you should be able to manage with one crutch when you go out of your room. When the cast is no longer necessary, you can go back to the cane. That will be about three weeks. Your assailants hit you precisely where you had been shot. It's as if they knew the right spot to inflict the maximum damage."

"It's so nice they were so accurate. How soon can I get out of here?"

"I need you to help me understand a few things."

"If I can."

"I am going to be brutally frank. I have to be, because you are in my care. I have two options of belief about you and the four murders. Either you know more about murders and disappearing drugs and money than you're telling me or you do not. I am not 100% convinced that you don't know what happened to the drugs and the money, which were in the parked car during shootout a few weeks ago. I am not totally convinced that you are just a witness.

If you know what happened to the merchandise and cash that would explain why the guys approached you at your home the other night and why you were attacked last night. It might also explain why you got only a whack on the leg and were not killed. The guys wanted to send a powerful warning. I might also explain why robbery was not a motive. They could have taken your wallet and split.

But, they spoke to you when you were on the ground. It might also explain why the two guys were yelling for you to return their merchandise.

Now, if you do know what happened to the merchandise, we need to know so we can get our hands on the stuff and use it to get the gang. Sure, we want the dealers. But, we really want their boss or bosses. You know, a lot of law-abiding people would look at you taking the coke and such as just a working stiff taking advantage of an opportunity that dropped in his lap. The guy who stumbled upon treasure buried by thieves many years ago. I'm sure the DA would not want to prosecute someone, who helped in such in high profile investigation regardless of what the individual may have found at a crime scene.

So, if you have any more knowledge of the missing coke and money and you gave me that knowledge, we could hide you away and use the merchandise as bait until this whole mess is resolved. Then you would be entitled to a big reward and public thanks. Maybe we would even forget there was money in the trunk at the murder scene."

"What the hell are you getting at, Willow?"

"It would not surprise me if you knew the exact whereabouts of the drugs. Whoever is getting information to Loco Lobos must believe the same thing. But, it doesn't matter where Loco Lobos got its information about you. They have it. And they are not going to let you alone until you return their stuff or tell them who has it. Up to now they have menaced you. Next they will take severe steps. They may go after your son. They will get your attention and you will do as they want, because business is business. And, you put a serious crimp in theirs.

They can't have that. First, they don't like to lose income. But, more important, they don't appreciate being disrespected in public. If a private citizen can thumb his nose at the Loco Lobos and get away with it, any street punk will think he can. And that's not good for their business both short-term and long-term."

"What does all this have to do with my being at the wrong place at the wrong time, the thinly veiled threat at my home, and the attack on me in the parking lot?"

"Jesus, man, are you dense? Or do you think me stupid? Although there is no absolute proof, they are convinced that you know where the drugs are. And I believe they are right. They will do anything to get them back and to show that they will not tolerate interference in their activities. As a last resort, they will kill the thief, who took their merchandise and write-off the lost revenue. They'll dump the poor bastard in the bay after they cut off his fingers and gouge out his eyes. He'll be alive when he enters the water, but not when we find him. But, they will do this only as a last resort. Before they do this they will exhaust all avenues to get back their goods. What you have experienced so far is only one avenue. If you don't help us, we can't help you. We can't protect you and you're gonna die. I can't stop them if you won't cooperate."

"I'm innocent of the theft you and the gang lay on me. But, until they can be brought to justice, I demand more protection. That's your job. Protect me. You know *Protect and Serve*."

"OK. We'll protect you. Put you under security so tight they won't be able to get to you. Security so tight you won't be able to take a pee without us knowing. While you're being watched we will use our usual sources to find the drugs and trace them back to the gang. With no help from you. Let me layout the scenario for you. I know you have taken a house in the country. The house has three bedrooms, one for you, one for your son, and a guestroom.

Well, you're going to get a guest for the third bedroom. Someone who will look and act like your roommate. I have secured the services of federal agent. This agent will be with you 24/7 even when your son is visiting. The agent will live at your house, share in the kitchen duties, buy groceries, and help with the cleaning . . . even get to know your son. The agent has been educated in telemarketing and will apply for work at your place. So you can't escape the agent."

"Wait. A live-in federal agent. Isn't that extreme? I was thinking about surveillance."

"You want protection. You scream for protection. And now you don't like it. Excuse me, sir, but you have no choice. Lieutenant Rodriguez and Captain Jacobs have assigned me to this case exclusively. This is my baby. This is my expressway to becoming a Lieutenant and then Captain . . . It was our joint decision to give you maximum protection until the investigation is over. But, to keep you visible to the public. No one else on the force knows of our plan or will be involved until the Captain, Lieutenant and I decide to involve them.

Because of the investigation's scope and complexities, as well as our need for total secrecy, the Captain asked for help from the Federal Organized Crime Force. They are lending us an agent, who is unknown to law enforcement officials and criminals in this area. This agent has experience dealing with organized crime elsewhere. The agent reports to me. Any communications you would have with me must go through the agent. I am in charge of this joint local and federal effort."

"Jesus, protected bait. Like a carcass in a shark cage. Assuming I agree to this, when do I meet the secret agent"?

"Later today. And your agreement is not necessary. We need to protect you and we need to follow the trail of drugs and money up the ladder . . . with or without your help. Consider the agent a babysitter. You two will meet as soon as you can get out of here. The agent will come to your house. The agent's name is Jonny Rivers. On second thought you do have an option. If you don't like this arrangement, we can move you to Santa Fe, New Mexico for a year or two. Without your son. He'll never know where you have gone. It'll be like you deserted him."

"Thanks for nothing."

With the wrap and a light, protective fiberglass cast, negotiating in and out of the car was as difficult as driving. But, I managed. Thank God for the automatic transmission. At home for two hours and no agent. I want this waiting over with now. Where is he? Knocking at the door confirms that wishing will make it so.

"Mr. Kermasic, I'm Jonny Rivers. I believe Officer Anthony Willow informed you that I would be arriving today."

"Office Willow told me that I needed a roommate. He didn't say anything about it being a woman. May I see some identification?"

"Sure."

It's all there on the identification badge. Ms. Jonny Rivers. Federal Number R-888729.

"May I see your driver's license and another piece of identification?"

The Florida license confirms she is the same person as on the Federal ID. The MasterCard corroborates the signature. She is either legit or a well-camouflaged Trojan Horse.

"May I see your sidearm?"

"You're skeptical. That's good."

She opens her duffel bag and extracts a 9mm Glock. I don't know if she should be carrying this piece or not, but my bluff worked.

"Now where can I stow my clothes and gear."

"Upstairs. I'd show you, but I can't do stairs very well."

For a few days she will stay in David's room. Tomorrow, Agent Rivers and I have to go furniture shopping for her real room. I hope her MasterCard will hold the purchases.

"What do I call you, Miss?"

"Jonny. Never Agent Rivers, Mr. Kermasic."

"Then you must call me Jerry. We have to give the appearance of friendship. The kitchen is complete and there's food for breakfast. I rarely eat lunch and never dinner at home unless my son, David, is with me. Did Officer Willow tell you about my son?"

"Yes, I have been thoroughly briefed. But, I would appreciate all other background information about him, his habits, and your relationship."

"Relationship. That's a good word. Just what is ours supposed to be?"

"I am a roommate. We are friends from work. I needed a place to stay because my previous roommate is getting married and moving out. You needed help with the expenses of getting the household up and running. It was a bit more than you could afford. This is an arrangement of short-term convenience. That's it."

"Then how will I explain you always being with David and me when we go out?"

"For a few weeks, you will be too cash-strapped to go out. You will stay at home for the next four or five weekends. Fish. Watch TV. Do what ever you want. Just do it on the property. Consider this to be safe haven for both you and David. As long as you are here with me, they can't get to you."

"How wonderfully disconcerting. I have a neighbor, who seems to be starved for friendship. Bob Potter and his son tend the groves. He has invited David and me to go fishing on the lake. Potter will probably be surprised by your sudden arrival. The people who own the house notified him of my move in. The lease makes no mention of a second adult. He'll be nosey."

"We'll deal with that in the normal course of events. Same story as with David. Consistency is critical. Can't let the story trip us up. OK?"

"So far, so good. Let's go out for dinner. I don't have the energy for cooking and it would be rude of me to impose upon you given this is your first day. You can cook, can't you?"

"Yes, I can cook and perform all of the other domestic chores required to maintain a household. We can split these up so they're not a burden. Given your leg. I'd be willing to assume all the chores for a few days. Sharing also creates the right impression. Tomorrow, I must go to Sun Shine and apply for work. I'll work on your shift so we're never apart. Protection is my job. Your safety is my purpose. Where would you like to eat?"

"Italian?"

"Great. Where?"

"The Italian Kitchen is a nice little place on Hillsborough. More than pizza and spaghetti."

"Can you drive with that bum leg?"

"Sure, but it's cumbersome and tiring. If you want to acclimate yourself to the neighborhood, you can drive. I'll navigate."

She drives a Jeep Wrangler. We bounce out the driveway to our culinary castle. The bouncing causes my leg to throb. I interrupt the uneventful business meal during my third glass of wine and one pain pill. This federal babysitter is almost attractive. Almost except for her attitude and intrusion into my life. Trim shape. Solid torso. The obvious manifestation of youth and hours at the gym. Dark hair with hues of red. Grey eyes and clear skin. Small nose and ears. Her smile is perfunctory, reacting to my comments, lame jokes, and feeble probes.

"How's the Tortellini?"

"Nice. The cream sauce is pleasant. And your Lasagna?"

"A little too much. I should have suspected it. This place has a reputation for stuffing its clientele.

I need to know how we are supposed to act when we're together so that I don't do something beyond the expected and blow your cover."

"We are a couple of friends, not a couple. If you keep that one thought always in your mind, you won't go wrong. I am with you, because it's my job. A job, for which I have been well trained. I was selected for this assignment, because I fit a specific profile. I have been thoroughly briefed about you and this case. There is no need for you to know anything about me other than I will be with you until there is a positive resolution of the investigation. I will accompany you wherever you go. I will protect you if the gang attempts to confront you. If they contact you in any way when you are out of my presence, you must share that information with me so that I can relay it to Officer Willow."

"So, I am bait."

"We prefer to consider your situation as cooperative protective custody. You're only bait, as you call it, because we believe you have not shared with us all the information about the murders and disappearance of the drugs and money. Hopefully, you will see the wisdom of sharing this information, and we can resolve the case faster than the tried and true hunt and arrest method. In the meantime, if, as you profess, you have no new information and the bad guys believe otherwise, they will continue to reach out to you. When they do, we will grab them up. Then you can go about your life."

"OK. Enough of the shoptalk. What about you? College? Family?"

"That's on a need to know basis, and you don't need to know."

"That slamming noise you just heard was the iron door closing the lines of friendly communication between us, and the crushing of my heart."

I sulked.

"As you wish. I said before, and now you understand, this is business. Business for me involves risk. To minimize risk, I must be singularly objective. There can be no personal niceties. Do you want dessert or can we leave?"

The ride home is icy. The wine and codeine tablet have reduced the pain and dulled my brain. I get the distinct impression that I touched a nerve beneath her all-business façade. In bed I have reminiscent feelings of my marriage. Here I am a healthy adult male under the same roof is a healthy adult female, to whom I am oddly attracted. I can't touch her. She made that very clear. She rejected me. I can't even display any form of affection. We must present to society at large the picture of a couple of friends sharing an abode but not life. I did this for two years and it tore me apart. The emotional stress of this situation could be devastating, if I let it. Certainly she won't. These are her inflexible rules.

* * *

Monday, we shop for her bedroom furniture. Delivery Tuesday. She goes to Sun Shine for a job application and interview two hours before I go to work. Her on-the-job-training was immediate. Monitoring calls. Studying the script. She leaves at six. So much for my protection. She's off the job the first day. It's a tough list, but the callers have good credit cards. The calls have to be worked long and hard. The day shift pulled 17 deals and two *deeks*. The room chatter is incessant and repetitious.

"Ma'am we are regulated by the Florida Department of Commerce. They approve our offers and how we promote them. Last week, when they were here, they gave us a commendation for positive business conduct."

"Your credit card protects you. We work through them and they work for you. The amount of $599 won't appear on your statement until well after you have received package of material. Then you can make your decision without spending any money. Does that sound fair?"

"The $2500 savings is our way of introducing our services to you. We are sure once you've tried Sun Shine Travel Services, you'll want us to be your regular travel agent."

"Is your wife at home with you now? Ask her to get on the other phone so I can explain the details of the tremendous offer to both of you at the same time. This is truly a once-in-a lifetime opportunity."

"What about saving over $2500, getting eleven days vacation, a cruise and a free rental car, do you not like?"

"If you're afraid your Visa card won't hold the amount, we can split the nominal fee between two cards."

"Why would you want to return your award and give up $2500 in savings, twelve nights of vacation, a free cruise, and a free rental car?"

"Discover cards are backed by Sears. They are the most difficult cards to get. The credit restrictions are tighter than MasterCard or Visa. Also, Sears' guidelines for businesses like ours are the most stringent. Sears monitors us daily. They may be listening to this call. But, the good news is that both you and Sun Shine have passed the tests of Sears. So we can do business together with all the safety, assurances, and protection of Sears. I believe your Discover card starts with a 6."

"If you hang up now, you'll lose this wonderful opportunity. While we will take your call back, your award will have been de-listed. I locked other award winners out of your award when I went into the mainframe at the beginning of this call. But if you hang up without securing your award, it will be made available to someone else. Your award is yours and yours alone with this one call. You'd like to look at all the material and discuss it with your husband, wouldn't you?"

"You can pay off your MasterCard as you want. The choice is yours. Pay it off before you take your vacations . . . $100 a month for six months. Then you can go on the vacations as if they were free."

The drill and drone never change. Two half-truths equal one lie. Get the card. Get the card. Get the card. Or fail, fail, fail. I get only one and it's already 8. Need a break. Hobble outside to the smokers.

"Jerry the K, how things goin'?"

"Jimmy the B, shittee."

"I got two solid and maybe a third, if the asshole doesn't kick. Hey, did you see the new trim scopin' out the biz tonight. Check her out."

"Saw somebody. Not sure who it was or what she was doin'."

"Looks like fresh meat for the night crew."

Badger would like to get a closer look at the new thang. Up close and very personal. After work. Maybe my place. Make you a bet. Bet I can score with the new flesh before anybody else. Whadda ya say? Twenty?"

"Before the bet. Did it ever occur to you that she might be from corporate or worse, from the State's Attorney General's office? Listening to you throw heat. Building a case to get your ass fired or fined."

"Nah, she's too cute for that. Body nice and trim. Solid. The way Badger likes it. Checked out her nails. They were short, dirty, and unpolished. If she was a spy, her nails would be nicer than that. They would be the nails of an office worker. Got the skinny from her app that she is a single mother. Debbie Grande. Big Debbie. Little body. Works mornings at some bank clearing house. Has prior telemarketing experience . . . customer complaints and selling warrantee contracts on appliance purchases. She's ripe for Badger. Wanna' bet?"

"OK, smart ass, I'll go twenty. But first, there has to be a time limit."

"Two weeks."

"Two weeks it is. You're on."

The balance of the night is fruitless. Badger's third kicks. He is pissed and slams his headset against the cube.

Pete sends him home. No place for violent reactions. Pete must be in control. The drive home is a pleasant decompression despite the awkwardness of the cast. As I turn into the drive, I realize I am being followed. They found out where I live.

Agent Rivers' car is not parked at the house. She deserted me on the first day. Uneasiness gives way to panic. Park around back. Out of the car and hop into the house through screened porch, I grab a carving knife and serving fork. The form approaches the door and giggles the handle. Then a key is inserted and the door opened. I am ready for the attack.

"Easy, Jerry, it's just me."

"Jesus-H-Christ, you scared the shit out of me. Where did you go tonight? You left me alone at work. Did you see the bastard who was following me home?"

"Slow down and listen. I never left you at work. I was in the parking lot two cars away from yours. It was me who followed you home. I told you at the beginning, I would protect you because that's my job. Now relax and go to bed. I will be upstairs. And I'm a light sleeper."

"Wait a fucking minute. When you leave me, like you did at work, tell me where you're going. Tell me where you'll be. That way I won't get worried."

"Where I go and where I am when you can't see me is on a need to know basis . . ."

"And, I don't need to know."

"Correct, just know that you are never far from my sight."

"I need a drink. Care to join me?"

"No thanks. Not in the job specs. Besides, I like to run before the sun comes up and alcohol this late at night impedes that exercise. Good night."

"Night."

* * *

Her furniture arrives around ten. Her room has the look of an Army barracks. No hint of individuality. Nothing feminine about the bed and headboard, bureau, table and chair. All in knotty pine. Straight lines. No curves or design. The bed cover is dark gray and dark blue. No dust ruffle. The two framed posters are non-descript examples of form art. Maybe this is her personality. Utilitarian and easily transferable to another location.

"I have to go food shopping for the week. Given my leg problem, I need you to be my cart mate."

"Wouldn't miss it for the world."

"I'm open to suggestions for meals. David will be with me Saturday until Sunday night. So I have to plan meals for three this weekend rather than two. If you have any thoughts about activities for the three of us, let's get them on the table. Most important, I will need help explaining your presence."

"My food choices include chicken and pork. Pasta. Beans and rice. I'll even cook a meal, if it's OK with you. Activities could include fishing. We'll need to buy the gear. I like to fish. Maybe chores around the house. That way your son will get a feeling of my contributing to his new home.

Movies are out. Too solitary for the presence of a non-family member. Miniature golf is a possibility. Except for your leg. You might want to explain to your son that you could not afford to set up this house without financial aid. You seriously underestimated all the costs in completing the household. Tell him that I will not be staying much longer than six months. I will be moving out of state to be with my parents. I need a short term, inexpensive place. It just worked out."

* * *

Tuesday callers, at least mine, seem to be more willing to purchase over the phone. I get two. Debbie Grande gets her first deal in the second hour and earns a $20 on-the-spot cash bonus. Everybody applauds. The galley slaves welcome the initiated. Wednesday is better. Get two by 8. Jimmy waves to me to take a break.

"Well things look bleak for Badger."

"Why, the list is good."

"Not the list, bum wad. The dolly. She has rejected my offers. Spurned me. Tells me she has to get home to her boy. She is working two jobs for now to pay off some bills her ex-husband left her. She is not too pleased with him. Maybe she's a dyke. Or turned because she got shat upon. Maybe that's why her old man split. Found her munching some carpet and called it quits."

"Badger, your imagination is working OT. Maybe she doesn't want to go out with you. May be it's you. Or maybe she really wants to take care of her son. Maybe you ought to give it a rest. Give me the twenty and call it quits."

"Fuck you asshole. I'll score with the dolly or confirm her dykieness. No chick can refuse Badger, once his mind is set upon her moistness. If she's straight that is."

"Well you still have ten days until you have to pay up."

"Hey, man can you get me eight by Friday's shift?"

"Sorry, Badger, my man has gone dry. He claims he'll have a stash by next weekend. Then we'll all get high."

"Man, my boys are jonesin'. We need and we need bad. Price is not a problem."

"Sorry, no gots."

"Contact your man tonight and double-check. We'll go $100 for the same quality stuff. Do it for Badger. And Badger will do props for you later."

"OK, I'll call him. But, he already told me he is not holding. So don't get your hopes up. Back to the fish."

* * *

The lead story in Metro Section of Thursday's newspaper wraps up my near fall.

Tampa Ledger May 13, 2013
Coed Dealer Busted

Last night, local Police and members of the Drug Enforcement Agency arrested Ashley Branson Rykes on the university campus, confiscated forty-seven grams of cocaine, and broke up a drug distribution ring, which included numerous students and two faculty members. Ms. Rykes blah, blah, blah . . .

With all the money and political juice behind her, she'll get off with a suspended sentence, rehab and some community service. The two professors will be canned and barred from any future teaching jobs. Ah, how the rich are protected and the non-rich get screwed.

VII

Badger is pissed that I can't deliver. His attitude is: *I ask. You deliver.*

"My man told me next week we will all feel good. Badger, I got a question. If somebody knew something about the murders and the allegedly missing drugs, how would that person get the information to the proper authorities . . . not the cops?"

"Why ask me? Do you think I have a pipeline?"

"I don't think you have a pipeline. I just thought you might know someone, who knew someone, who could direct a person to the right person to talk to."

"Whatever this person may know, he can tell me. Then I'll ask around to see if this information is of interest to anybody. There are no guarantees, you realize. I just know some people, who might know some people, who might be interested in learning what happened to the alleged drugs and money."

"I'll see if this person would like to talk to you."

"Yeah, you do that."

He is suspiciously pissed.

The callers have opened up their wallets. Rather than five or six rebuttals, the credit cards numbers spew forth after two or three. The fish are jumping into the boat. Everybody will make quota. The new girl gets two before the West Coast callers kick in. Jackie is working her back seat business. One by one the guys take smoke breaks with her. She'll make more on her knees than any one can sitting in a cube. Shift over. Clock out. Head for home. My shadow is within sight. Must find a way to get to U-Stor-It for cash. Can't touch the nose candy, at least for the time being.

* * *

"Well, Jonny, how did you like your first week?"

"Very interesting."

I see her shoulders relax and a small smile appears.

"Would you like a celebratory drink? Just one."

"Sure. Do you have any scotch?'

"No, but I have two bottles of Scot's Whiskey . . . Ushers for every day and Balvenie for celebrations. I'll get the Balvenie. How do you like it?"

"Water and one cube. A lot of water."

"You passed that test."

"What?"

"You failed the name portion of the exam, but on the consumption portion you got a solid B."

We sit at the kitchen table, which is also the dining table. Glasses clink.

"Tell me about this guy Jimmy Monteleone."

"Jimmy's nickname is Badger, which is they way he treats the callers and anyone else he thinks appropriate. He is telehuckster from the get go. Normally at the top of sales. Always highest on the kick list. These people will buy just to get him off the phone, and then they will reject the sale through the credit card within 48 hours. That's about it for Badger."

"Is there a Mrs. Badger or a Badgerette?"

"Very clever. No. I doubt if a woman could stay with Jimmy more than the five minutes he finds necessary for his physical gratification. Why do you ask?"

"He's been hitting on me. It's happened before. I know how to deal with guys like him."

"Be careful. Badger does not take well to rejection. There have been situations where he has become abusive on the phone and Pete has had to send him home. Be judicious as to how you rebuff him."

"I've see you two talking sometimes. What else do you know about him?"

"He's a local. Grew up in a tough neighborhood, but did not go tough. Just unpolished. Lives in a house with four other guys. Two work at corporate. One sells jewelry in the malls. The fourth works for the largest funeral home in the area picking up stiffs from homes and hospitals. Works when called. Lives a good life off what he lifts from the stiffs. I suspect the house is like a fraternity, except none of these guys went to college."

"Do you think he is connected?"

"No. But, it wouldn't be a shock if he knew someone at every level of Loco Lobos. Not to have dinner with, but he probably has been in their houses and seen them at big events."

"Do you think he knows more about the murders and drug deal then he is letting on?"

"Maybe. Yes. I have wondered why the deal was going down in the parking lot of our strip center. I know Jimmy uses, but so do a lot of guys in the business."

"Do you think he moves any weight?"

"Only enough for personal enjoyment, the enjoyment of his homies, and some chump change. It's not major weight. Maybe 6-8 grams a week. Depends on the buyers' cash flow, I guess."

"How about you?"

I change the subject from interrogation to social drinking.

"Yes, I'll have another. And how about you?"

"Yes, thanks. It tastes nice and smooth."

"How about you?"

She is back on the trail.

"What do you mean?"

"What I mean is do you move any weight?"

"Before I answer that question with a resounding *no fucking way*, let me weigh my options. Option one: If I do move weight, I will be arrested. Option two: If I don't move weight, I remain free. Arrested. Free. Arrested. Free. I choose free. No I don't move weight. Why do you ask?"

"Look, we're not looking to jam you up. We're looking to solve six murders and close down a drug ring. In an ideal world, we would like to follow the drug dealing up the ladder to Loco Lobos and close them down, too. Right now you are our best prospect for success. You were there. You know Jimmy. You can be a valuable asset. That's why we are protecting you. It's our way of showing we care. We would hope you would want to cooperate with us. You've seen how the other guys treat you. They shoot you and beat you. We are somewhat easier to work with."

A chill sets into my spine. The drinks are working on my mind. I pour two more.

"I mentioned to Badger that I might know somebody who might know something about the allegedly lost drugs and money. I asked him if he knew a way for this person to get this information to the right people. Of course, he wants all the credit. You know, tell him and he'll tell the guys. I told him that I would see how this mystery person felt."

"How do you feel?"

"Scared. The water is rising to my chin. If I don't swim soon, I'll drown."

"What do you know that you haven't told the police? You can tell me now and we can really help."

"What are you saying? You and I will do something about this situation. If we bring in Officer Willow and his storm troopers, their jackboots will muck up everything. Only we can protect me. I need you to promise that we are the team. We will take this thing to the next level and the level after that. And, maybe the one after that. When the fat lady is singing, we will let Willow in on our game. Deal?"

"Deal."

"One more thing. No judgment."

"OK."

I hope I can trust her. The facts flow faster than the next drink. I am getting the jack as I gain control of the situation. As I bring her in as my confidant, she must rely on me. Her eyes are steady, reflecting her mind and training. They soften, as she understands the financial pressure I was under and the opportunity the drugs provided. Like the piñata opened and all the goodies fell into my lap. She never changes expression with the details of the university distribution system. She is cool. Way cool. But, she winces at my bet with Badger.

"Twenty bucks. Is that all you think I'm worth? You will collect. But I want half the payoff for the rigged game. I agree that Jimmy is a good avenue to the gang. But, he and the process are very dangerous. What exactly did you have in mind to tell the bad guys?"

"I was going to tell them that I could get their drugs and money back for them. I didn't have the stolen goodies, but could convince the person who did have them to turn them over to their rightful owners. For safety, this person has to remain anonymous. I'd would just leave the merchandise somewhere for the guys to pick up."

"What if you told Jimmy the he is a she? That would throw suspicion off you."

"OK. Then what?"

"We set a trap at the drop. This will require Officer Willow. He has the resources to pick up the men, who will roll on their bosses. Or, he just follows the merchandise back to the big guys. It's his choice. You and I are out of it then. Reasonable?"

"But, I thought we agreed to keep him out of it until the A-team had done its job."

"This is our job. Set up the delivery and walk. OK? There is a risk that, if the returned merchandise is not exactly what the owner expect they could be very pissed. Do you understand?"

"Yes and no."

"I mean, you told me you were dealing off their stuff. They will expect the return of all the stolen drugs or the cash equivalent."

"Not possible."

"How much is left of the original weight?"

"Less a kilo and a half. There was a little less than two kilos when I came into possession. Plus, about $6000."

A small lie.

"How much did you deal?"

"The balance of what is missing."

"Then you have the cash."

"Not all of it."

"At $80 per gram, you should have a bundle. How much do you have?"

"I'd have to check the box. I know there is some cash. I just don't know how much."

"There better be a lot of cash. Or, you're in deep shit."

"I got an idea. Let's give them back everything they expect. We step on what's left. Not a big step. Just enough to make up what was dealt. Then we turn over the unsold coke and some cash. They'll be none the wiser. The people who buy the stuff on the street have no benchmark of comparison."

I failed to mention that I would keep some cash as payment for my end.

"If, before the put it on the street, they figure out that you returned inferior goods, they'll come after you. I'll be out of town by then. So the risk is all yours. I can't help you if you chose to go that route. But, if you decide to do that, Tony Willow will have to know so he can hide you."

"I don't have much choice. I dealt enough of their weight to get me in a world of hurt. I hope that Tony Willow and his cavalry come riding over the hill before the bad guys realize they have been had. If Willow doesn't arrive before the epiphany, I'm fucked."

"It's your choice, but Tony must know what you plan to do. Your actions will influence his."

"I'll think about what I want to do. In the mean time, I'll get back to Badger and tell him about the bad person that has the drugs. Should we set up a meeting between the bad girl and the bad guys?"

"Yes, I need visual identification to be used later in court. You will not be at the meeting. But, someone else will be watching you. Now, I need to go to bed. This whiskey has wrecked me."

Jonny pulls herself up from the chair and slowly navigates the stairs.

"Do you need any help?"

"You and your crutch help me? Not on your life. Oops, bad choice of words."

She is giggling.

"Seriously, I can manage. No work tomorrow, right?"

"Right."

"Then wake me before noon . . . just before noon."

A burden has been shared and lifted from my shoulders. Now I have new issues and a new burden. But, I am back in the hunt and not the hunted. Somehow the thrill of the hunt minimizes its inherent danger and the discomfort of stair climbing. The building or rebuilding is more exhilarating than the edifice. Sleep is sound.

* * *

The alarm follows the sun by one hour. The first of two days with David. This will be a great weekend. Jonny is on the back porch with a mug of coffee. I introduce them. David understands the need for a temporary roommate. He fully understands my strong aversion to debt.

I never realized how much was involved in fishing. Whatever happened to the pole, string, bent pin, and worm of Rockwell's painting? Three basic outfits are carried to the dock. Our lunch is a break for the fish . . . they can stop laughing at our ineptness. The afternoon's piscatorial assault is for my son and me. Jonny has volunteered to prep dinner. Her treat. Putt-Putt golf must wait for Sunday, if I have the strength.

The fresh air, cool for this time of year, takes its toll on both father and son. The pork, rice and pinto beans in a molasses, mustard and bay sauce is enough to leaden the eyelids. The two drinks help me. The chef graciously volunteers to handle KP. I can't carry David upstairs. Hell, I can barely help myself. Sunday is a repeat of the good feelings. David is home by eight. I am home by nine.

* * *

The good list is dead. The bad list rules. Damn this is a B week. Time for the thermal ray gun or a mega flamethrower. Without a deal, I take an early break.

"Badger, how goes the hunt?"

"Hunt the cunt. She is nowhere to be found. The telephone number I glommed off the app is answered by a machine. She never calls back. I'm going to have to move tonight. Put the heat to the honey. She'll fold."

"Ever the optimist. By the way, I spoke to my friend and my friend would like to meet with your friends whenever you can arrange it . . . if you can."

"Tell this guy, I'm not sure I can reach out to my friends for an unknown. He must go through me."

"My friend does not want to go through you. My friend will meet directly with your friend. My friend wants all the props. My friend did the deed and wants to demonstrate contriteness. You'll get your props, because your friends will know who made the introduction. My friend wants more than just a second hand thank you. My friend may have an ulterior motive for meeting your friends. Like a business relationship."

"Tell him. No me. No meet."

"My friend thought you'd say that. My friend's response is sorrow you feel that way. But, there are other ways to get to your friends. Plus, your friends will learn that you knew about my friend all along. Then no props for you. You may even get a spanking for being a bad boy."

Badger's body stiffened. His jaw jutted out and his eyes glared at me.

"Easy, Badger, I'm just the messenger. Don't get pissed at me. My friend said that if you were cooperative, made the right introductions, and did not insist on being at the meeting, my friend would reward you."

"OK. I don't like this, but I'll do it. My effort is worth 2 large. Tell your friend that I'll call him when the meeting is set. Give me his number."

"My friend said one large. Tell me when and where the meeting is. Then, I'll tell my friend. Then the two sides can meet. I'm out of the loop and you're out of the loop. Oh, Badger, bad luck on your conquest. Do you have the twenty?"

"Asshole."

Pitching heat is ever present.

"But, ma'am, if you don't secure your award with this phone call, you'll lose it. Now, your MasterCard starts with a 5."

"If you weren't interested in the eleven days of vacations, why did you call? You are interested, right?

Then let's get this package out to you tonight. Will you be using a Visa card?"

"Sir, the last four digits of your American Express card indicate your billing cycle. If you'll just read me the last four digits, I can tell you when the promotional fee will appear on your statement. Great. Those numbers tell me that the service fee won't even go onto your bill for three weeks from next Wednesday. That's well before you'll get the package of material. So you can decide where you want to go first. Now, what are all the numbers on the card?"

"If you chose to cancel your award after you've reviewed all the material, you are protected by your credit card. So, I'd like to send the material. Which credit card will you be using?"

"Do I hear you saying that you don't want to save over $2500, get twelve days vacation, a free cruise, and a rental car? Of course you like saving money. It's the American way. Will you be securing the vacations with your MasterCard or Visa?"

"There is absolutely nothing to risk. Your credit card works for you and we work for your credit card. Will you be using a Visa Card or MasterCard?"

"You're actually being a smart shopper saving all that money. These are vacations your friends would pay over $5000 for including airfare. But, you have a chance to lock them in for less than $600. So, if you read me the numbers on your card, we will express the material to you. You'll receive the package in two days."

"This is our special spring promotion and is approved by the Florida Department of Tourism and Travel. If you read me the numbers on your credit card, I can secure your vacations and send you the lovely material."

"The State Attorney General uses our operation as a model for the travel industry. We accept all major credit cards and have received endorsements from them all."

We're all sweating bullets. Getting the cards is like trying to change a tire on a moving car. At the end of the evening, here are only 12 deals on the board. I got zapped. Home to lick my wounds.

* * *

"I made contact with Badger. He was not in a very good mood. First, he can't reach you so he can't score. Second, the list is the pits. Third, he doesn't like the idea of just being a hands-off matchmaker. He wants to meet my friend, and take my friend to the guys. I told him my friend wanted no part of an escort. So, Badger is to set up the meet, tell me, and my friend would appear. Jimmy doesn't know if I have a friend or if the source of knowledge is me. He doesn't even know if my friend is male or female. I kept all reference gender neutral. But, I think he suspects me. We must decide who goes to the meeting. But, he wants his grand up front."

"No decision necessary. I go. I can be an expert witness. Your testimony could be compromised by your illegal actions up to this point. Argument settled. I'll have the grand whenever the meeting is set."

I hated that type of finality. Hated all during my marriage. It's as if my comments don't count. That I don't count. It trivializes me. It minimizes me. Makes me very angry. Petulantly destructive.

"So it's agreed. When Badger tells you of the meeting, you'll tell me, and I'll go alone."

"What if they grab you up then and there and try to beat the information from you?"

"That is not in their best interest. Their business interests are best served by retrieving the merchandise and the money. Only then am I in real danger. My usefulness as a courier is over. Their next step is to make a spectacle of me. Something they can hold up to all concerned as to how they deal with business interlopers. That's why I turn the affair over to Tony and I leave town."

"I feel rejected. Like an old toy."

"We wouldn't be having this conversation if you hadn't been at the wrong place at the wrong time. That's an unfortunate fact of fate. But, issue became complicated when you were recognized. Then, you created a problem by stealing the money and drugs. Your actions after your stole the stuff compounded the problem . . . made the hole deeper. Further fuck-ups on your part and you'll be covered with dirt and given a headstone. Why do you want to continue this charade? You are not the hero. You are a private citizen, who tried to exploit a bad situation and by doing so made it worse. So back off and do as you are told. I'm here to protect you and bring this situation to a positive resolution with no loss of life. Let me do my job. Now, to a more pleasant subject: work."

Her abruptness and subject change caught me off guard.

"What about it?"

"The operation is unethical."

"Oh, really. Over the edge illegal is more like it. Here's how it works. We sell the vacation packages to unsuspecting fish. The vacations are really come-ons underwritten by time-sharing organizations. We never mention that. The value of the rooms, cruise, and car rental is about $200 at supplier cost. Sun Shine gets about

$350 of the $599. The telehuckster gets $50. When the fish calls to make reservations, he is pushed to upgrade. Goaded, prodded, and lied to some more. The reservation desk people make big money getting the fish to upgrade. About one-fifth of the upgrade. They use all types of excuses. The hotels the fish thought he had are either under renovation or there is a surprise convention. The reservation clerk can get the fish into a new luxury room for a little more.

Upgrades on the total package average at $500. Then there are the fees, taxes and charges. These amount to about $350. The port fee actually pays for the cruise. Somehow the fish never was told about these. But, these charges are just governmental levies, so the fish is told. Meals and incidentals for two run $1800 for the ten days. Nothing is cheap in the resort. Then there's transportation. Depending on the time of year the vacations are taken, and most are planned for the prime winter season, airfare for the complete package can run $3000. So, if a couple really wants to take the vacations, they will spend about $6000 dollars. Six large so that they can be hounded by the time-share sharks. If you think we're ruthless, you ought to see the sales people at the resorts. All along the fish thought they were spending only $599 for three luxury vacations. It's a big con."

"Then why do you do it?"

"The money is decent for the hours required. Some weeks the fish are biting and the harvest is good. Some weeks we have to lie to close the deal. Plus, the owner is paying me a special way. For weeks 1,3,5,7 etc, I am paid for my deals, with the appropriate taxes taken out. For weeks 2,4,5,8 etc, which always include a Saturday, I receive a payroll check for my quota of twelve, if I make the deals, which I do. And for any deals above twelve I am paid in cash in a separate envelope. Can't sneeze at two yards from Mr. Green."

"Does he do this for everybody?"

"Don't know. Don't care. Hey, you're not going to report this to the IRS are you?"

"No, they have enough to do without chasing after little players like you and your boss."

"Thanks for the kind words. But, the underlying reason I'm here is that during the day hours I am able to look for work in my chosen profession, which is legitimate marketing. I view this stint with Sun Shine as a brief tour of duty. In country, as it were. There has got to be something better. Beyond all that, if I weren't here I would have never seen the shoot out, found the drugs, and met you."

"I'll bet you say that to all your body guards."

"Only the women. Now that you've seen mine, show me yours."

"It's none of your concern."

"The hell it's not. I didn't get a chance to interview you or check your credentials. How can I be sure you're up to the task? Would you take a bullet for me?"

"You have to go on faith. Faith that the local and federal authorities feel this case is big enough to devote manpower, money and resources to solve it. Faith that Tony Willow and Jonny Rivers will hitch their careers to this star. When we are successful, we will be rewarded. To be successful, we have to make every effort to protect you. Satisfied?"

"Have you protected other witnesses before me?"

"No."

"Great, a bossy, know-it-all virgin queen, is sent to protect me from the evil emperor. A virgin who claims to have the wits and magic sufficient to defeat a force that is larger, more powerful and wiser than she. That's fucking reassuring."

"If you'd rather go this alone . . . with no help from Willow or me, we will back off. Before you go there, think of David. If you fail to deliver, these thugs would not think twice about grabbing him and using him as leverage to get the information from you. Once they have what they need they would have to clean up. The cleaning would involve the disappearance of you and your son. So, the choice is quite simple. Go with us and protect your son. Or, be a macho asshole and lose two lives. Gee, that choice seems easy to make even for you."

"Answer me one thing. Are you guys watching out for David?"

"Should we?"

"Fuck you, bitch."

Trapped, I storm off to bed.

VIII

Café Centro Real is alive. Saturday morning is for friends and business associates to enjoy Cuban coffee and Cuban toast while they share the week's joys and travails, and personal glimpses into their families. The rich and spicy aromas wash away any ills of the immediate past and stimulate the olfactory senses with the promise of satiety. Breakfast is an all morning event, which blends into lunch and afternoon coffee. This ritual is essential to sustain the Hispanic community's traditions and build its future.

The men are dressed in khakis and white guaveras. Black shoes, lace ups . . . no sandals, and white socks. Never hats. Hair and moustaches range from black through henna to white. Gold jewelry . . . watches, necklaces, and teeth, never earrings. The sameness of the population is manifested in its collective stature: rarely over 5'8" and slightly overweight for the men under 50 and underweight for the elders.

This group ebbs and flows in two modes: from table to table, as well as in and out of the café. The tile floor, absence of wall covering, and cathedral ceiling amplify the nattering, as well as the clinking of the plates, cups and saucers. Floor to ceiling windows on three walls are the primary sources of light. Flickering fluorescent tubes backlight the kitchen and the long tables, which hold the food and coffee. Tables, set up in an orderly fashion at 5 AM, have long since been moved twice to accommodate the ebb and flow of the breakfast club. There are no two-tops.

Four-tops have been joined for eight, or twelve. Then the tables have been reconfigured for a new crowd. There are two booths on each of the two sidewalls. None on the wall looking onto the patio. The two corner booths accommodate different clusters: one the elders' elders and the other one middle-aged man and two younger women. The only women in the café. This is the target booth.

"Good morning, sir, my name is Jonny Rivers. I'm a friend of Jimmy Monteleone."

"I don't know who you're talking about. I don't know any Jimmy Monteleone."

"I'm sorry, sir. I thought Jimmy Monteleone had arranged a meeting for today. A meeting in which I could discuss the return of some lost merchandise. Merchandise, which, I was lead to believe, belonged to you or someone you know. I guess I am mistaken. Sorry for the intrusion."

Jonny turns slowly and walks with casual deliberation through the front double door. The bait has to be taken away from the fish. The objective of the exercise is for the fish to swim faster and bite harder on the bait and hook once it has been taken away. At the intersection cross walk, Jonny feels a tug on her arm. She spins prepared to defend herself against attack. One of the women from the booth smiles.

"Please come back, Mr. Smith would like to talk to you."

Before Jonny can sit in the booth, she is not very discreetly patted down. The massaging of her breasts and stroking of her mons are not necessary. But, the blonde seems to enjoy it. Jonny's back stiffens and she clenches her teeth. The blonde nods to Mr. Smith.

"Miss . . .

"Rivers, Jonny Rivers."

"My apologies for the confusion. I was the one who was mistaken. I was expecting to meet a man not an attractive woman."

"Well, Badger incorrectly assumed and you know that makes an ass out of you and me."

"Badger, as you call him, is a good boy. Not brilliant. And certainly not level headed. But, he does follow orders and he is the face of the future."

"Yes, a not-so-brilliant future leader. How sad. Now about this merchandise. I understand you're looking for it."

"Ah, yes, the merchandise that was stolen from us. I hate thievery. Don't you Miss Rivers? In a business world, there is no room for thieves. Thieves are like vultures. No, they are lower than vultures. They are weasels that steal eggs from a nest. Don't you agree?"

"Yes, thieves are the lowest. But, an opportunist or an entrepreneur is held in much higher esteem. Someone who takes advantage of a situation and profits from it is not a thief, but is a clever business person."

"Opportunist. Is that what you call someone who takes what is not his and disposes of it for a profit? Is he an entrepreneur? I think not."

Mr. Smith sits high on the booth bench. His long black hair shines. The braided rat-tail is about six inches long. No moustache. His shoulders are broad and chest thick from working out. He does not wear a guavera. Rather, he has adorned his torso with a snug fitting medium yellow and white silk blouse, no collar, buttoned to the throat and short sleeved. His understated Swiss wristwatch and simple gold ring on his left pinky are expensive adornments. No earrings. His nails reflect weekly manicures. Skin tanned naturally. Gray eyes and well-capped teeth. A comely appearance.

The blonde to his right and the brunette to his left wear no make up. Their hair is short, clean, and brushed back. Skin is clear. Each has hazel eyes. Their shoulders and arms are slightly overdeveloped. Their skin on their hands is chapped and nicked, and their nails are cut short . . . they are not polished. These two work outside with their hands. They have matching brown livery jackets over red men's shirts. No jewelry except for ear studs, a matching set on each, about the size of an index finger nail. The silver studs are in a lace pattern. Like a snowflake. Neither talks nor smiles.

"Sir, with no disrespect, our differing points of view have little to do with the transaction of returning your merchandise."

"I agree."

"Please understand that I do not know exactly where the merchandise is now, but my friend, who is in possession of the goods, has assured me that the goods can be delivered to you within twenty-four hours."

"Good."

"Unfortunately, my friend took the liberty of selling some of the merchandise. And then he spent the proceeds.

As a result, I have been informed that the count in the two bags of is less than when they were found. But, there is cash remaining from the sales."

"Let me get this straight. This punk, bastard took my candy, dealt it off, and then spent money, which is rightfully mine. He will have to make good or we will make his life over. How much did he move? How much money does he have?"

"I am not positive."

"I won't let some thief take my goods, use them, then return the unused portion for a full refund. In this case a walk. I want all my candy back and the money that was in the other bag . . . that's 10 large. Or, I want full restitution for the merchandise sold at $90 per. I estimate that to be 90 large per K. The total then is 200. As you can see, Miss Rivers, my goods are of great value."

"Sir, your math is intriguing. But, I'm not trying to negotiate for my friend. I believe the merchandise was sold for less that 90 each. But, I can see that you hold your merchandise in high regard."

"I want what is mine or the cash equivalent. 200. That's it. You see, Miss Rivers, I am a peaceful man, not given to violence. And I want to resolve this matter in a non-violent manner. But, if I don't receive restitution, I will send people to visit your friend. My people will get me satisfaction. As, I'm sure you can appreciate, it is bad for business to allow a thief to run free. It encourages others to try the same thing. This can lead to wholesale mayhem. No control. And there can be no business without control. So, it behooves me to nip this minor upheaval in its nascent stage. You know, before it takes on a life of its own. You can appreciate that, can't you"?

"Yes, I can. And you can rest assured that I will do everything in my power to make the situation right in your eyes."

"That's good. I think I can trust you, because you understand me."

"Yes I do, sir. Now, where would you like the merchandise delivered?"

"Tomorrow at five, have your friend bring the goods and cash back here. To this same booth. That's five sharp. Any delay, and I'll know your friend, and you too, can't be trusted. But, when this matter is resolved to my satisfaction, I'd like to give you a special thank you."

"Thank you. I'll make it happen. May I ask you something?"

"Yes."

"Who are these two? You are obviously a man of taste and polish. These two field hands are beneath you."

"Interesting choice of words . . . beneath me. That's good. These two ladies work for me. As I told you, we were expecting a man. I thought these ladies might have interested him. You know, sweeten the game. They were prepared to spend some time with this guy. Please him. And that now you know their purpose for being here would you be interested in spending some time on a Saturday afternoon with the two of them? As a pre-reward for helping me."

"Not my style. I prefer the old-fashioned arrangement. Besides, wouldn't the guns tucked into the backs of their belts get in the way?"

"Very astute Miss Rivers. I like that. I await your friend at five tomorrow. Good day."

Jonny is dismissed from the court with a whisk of the hand and flick of the wrist. She returns to her car in the most circuitous manner. Going through outdoor stalls and the back doors of two bars. Not followed. Great training.

* * *

"The original owner of the merchandise you stole calls himself Mr. Smith. He wants everything cleared up by Sunday at five. He wants goods and cash totaling 200 thousand. He values the grams at 90 each. Do you have anything near 200? How far off his mark are you?"

"Not far at all. Look I'll just do what I suggested. I'll step on the stuff until I can make enough to bring it and the cash up to 200."

"Why do I have an uneasy feeling about this?"

"You don't trust me, and that makes me sad. You don't trust yourself and that worries me. It's all a matter of trust. Here's what's going to happen. I am going to get the stuff, and some Italian baby laxative, a couple of boxes of Goodies Powder, and a box of those little plastic bags. I can mix the laxative and Goodies so that it looks like coke. Then mix this with the real stuff and re-bag it all. It will not be as high quality as the original, but no one at Mr. Smith's level will be the wiser. The dumb assholes, who buy the stuff on the street won't know they've been conned, because they have nothing to compare the new stuff with. It will be business as usual. You can deliver the stuff and the cash tomorrow. Officer Willow follows the merchandise from the café to Mr. Smith. He grabs the bad guys. Bingo, I'm off the hook. You leave town until the trial. We all live happily ever after."

"You get the merchandise and the other materials now. I'll call Tony and set up the drop and follow."

"I'll be back in about an hour."

Return seventy-six minutes later. The sweat is a manifestation of the panic. Must work hard to remain in control. She doesn't know how heavy the step has to be to create the total amount. Chase her out of the room while working. How the hell did this happen? Took from both bags and now have less than a kee and a quarter. The cash totals 25 large. Keep 10 for the aggravation. Going to have to really stomp on the shit to make it good for the owner. Oh, well, what the hell. My protection wears a bra and carries a 9mm. Better be prepared to disappear for two or three months just to be safe. David will understand after the fact. Maybe I'll take him with me. I'll explain it all.

The process begins. Weighing each bag makes it a slow process. I can cheat by sight matching a new bag with an old one. Four hours and the booty is ready.

"Let me see the bags of coke. They seem OK. A little battered is good given your handling of them. How much cash did you put in the third bag?"

"Fourteen, eight-fifty. The equivalent of the missing 165 grams"

"OK, give everything to me."

"Where are you going?"

"It's better that you don't know."

* * *

Jonny's drive to Tampa International Airport and back takes fifty-five minutes. The storage locker key is placed in an envelope. Her note says: *TIA. Delta Baggage Claim West. Locker Number 876.* The note and small envelope are placed in a standard envelope, which she seals with tape.

"Now what do we do?"

"I have this envelope delivered to the café. Mr. Smith sends his messengers to the airport. They pick up the bags. Then the local police will do their thing. In a perfect world the warrants have been issued and all the arrests will be made before Sunday midnight."

"So, we're out of the loop for now. We wait."

"You got it."

"You haven't told me about your meeting with Mr. Smith."

"That's right."

"Well, what happened?"

"Not much. He is much like all the other faux-sophisticated scum, who view their illegal activities as some form of legitimate economic endeavor. He oozed machismo and plastic charm. Tried to con me with how much he liked me. All the while he was sitting between two dyke hookers, who were packing. The entire day is enough to make me want a long hot bath, and sleep for twelve hours."

"Two dyke hookers?"

"Yeah, a blonde and a brunette. Outdoorsy types. Big shoulders and rough hands. He claimed to have brought them in case his guest was a guy. They were to screw his brains out, then get then information from him before they killed him."

"The characters of the play are being announced one-by-one."

"What's that supposed to mean?"

"Right before you were assigned to be my bodyguard, I was supposed to meet two women at the Holiday Inn for a night of frolic. It was then that I was jumped and beaten, and Officer Willow saved my ass. I had met these women a few weeks before that night at a local saloon. A saloon, not coincidentally, where Badger knew I would be. Shit I have been surrounded ever since the murders."

"Ever since you took the drugs and money. That's all very interesting ancient history. I'm going for a run. Then dinner. Then to bed. Sorry you can't join me?"

"I can be with you in two out of three?"

I tried my best little boy-pleading smile.

"One for three . . . dinner only. Hell a lot of grown men make a lot of money batting 333."

Jonny's scowl was mixed with a grin.

The testosterone of challenge was met with the estrogen of control. Sleep is fitful. Anticipating the actions and reactions of tomorrow, as well as the plethora of 'what ifs' keeps two bodies tossing and turning with no satisfaction. The morning and afternoon each are 24 hours long. The wait is crushing.

* * *

Tampa International Airport is uncommonly busy Sunday evening. Numerous planes have been endured initial departure delays so there is a very heavy load of incoming passengers between 4 and 8 PM. More than the usual load. The peak crush is around 6. Each of the Delta Baggage Claim Carousels conveys personal effects from four flights. The area is so crammed that the skycaps can't ply their trade with the speed necessary to make big money. Kids are crying and crawling. Grown men are growling. Women are pacing. The elderly, here for vacation, stand comatose in the corners. They know their bags will be the ones remaining. No sense fighting the jostling crowds.

Two women are leaning on the wall near locker 876. The crush of humanity ebbs and flows to them and from them. Passes them right. Passes them left. It requires the vantage points of two Skycaps, a custodian, a passenger, and the lost and found office, to keep the locker under constant surveillance. Tony Willow feels in control.

The two women approach the hot zone. The crowd rushes passed. The key is in the lock. The locker is emptied. The bait is gone.

"Bingo. Bingo. Bingo. The package has been snatched. Two females wearing brown jackets, jeans and riding boots are heading out the electric door. Runner One. Runner Two, do you copy?"

"Roger that Hunter. This is Runner One. I see the birds in flight."

"Runner Two. I spot the birds getting into a new Lexus. Four door. Black. License number LXT 4JY. I will follow."

"Runner One is behind Runner Two. We will flip flop to avoid detection. Hunter, follow our directions to the nest."

The three cars exit the airport and head across the big bridge toward Saint Petersburg. Down Fourth Street, six miles to 22nd, then north and east on to the interstate to Tampa. This dodge fools no one. The traffic is light.

"Runner Two, have you been made?"

"Nah, the birds are just very cautious. I would be, too. I mean, they just picked up 200 large from a public place. Caution is the better part of survival. They are turning off the Interstate at Gandy. Looks like they are heading west. Runner One, can you take over?"

"Roger that."

"The birds are doubling back onto the Interstate. They'll spot me for sure. Hunter can you follow them.

Roger that, One and Two. Pull behind me by half a mile. I have them in my sight."

The new bad-good-guy tandem travels to the Exit #4 in Tampa . . . 21st/22nd Street. Land of the Zone. The Lexus pulls up to Café Centro Real. One valet opens the passenger door and out slinks a dark haired, petite woman in a white sequined dress, lots of gold, and three-inch gold spiked FM shoes. From the driver's side strides Mr. Smith. Willow is crushed. He checks the license plate: IXJ 9TY. They've been had.

Jonny's face is ashen when she folds away her cell phone.

"Bad news."

"What happened?"

"The police lost the pick up."

"Explain."

"The cash and coke were in a locker at the airport. The stuff was picked up by two women. Probably your friends from the motel and my meeting with Mr. Smith. Somewhere between the airport and Café Centro Real the women changed cars and the police followed Mr. Smith to the café. The women got away. The drugs got away. The bait got away. Now we have no trail. Nothing to follow. The only good news is that Mr. Smith will be placated. I'm safe. You're safe. Officer Willow has to start on a fresh route."

"How did they know to switch? Did they know they were being followed?"

"Just general precaution, I guess."

"Now what? What about me?

"You will be safe. You weren't the one to make contact with Mr. Smith. You were the middleman. So it will be life as usual. Except there will be no me in your life. No on-site protection, because it won't be necessary. I'm out of here. My usefulness is spent until the case goes to trial. Then I'll come back to testify that I arranged the drop with Mr. Smith. I'll pack and be out of your way tomorrow."

"Must you leave so quickly? Can't you stay for a few days? Can't we get to know each other as people and not as a job?"

"No. That's not in my job specs. I was here to protect you and to facilitate a way to the top of the dung heap. My job included getting you to open up and cooperate with our investigation. I protected you. You opened up. You cooperated. It's just that the investigation came to a momentary hiatus. The investigation has no further need of my presence. You can now go back to your telemarketing and raising your son. I will be reassigned. Let's have a toast to a successful case closure."

Talk about feeling empty. All my future wrapped up in the coke and cash has disappeared. Caused by the scum who was trying to push it. The thrill of the case . . . white hats against black hats . . . is over. The hint of the social conquest of Ms. Rivers has disappeared in the breeze that brought her here and now takes her away. The most exciting thing now for me will be to extract credit card numbers from the unsuspecting, unwashed middle-class. I feel I've been violated and robbed.

But, they didn't get it all. The process of rebuilding can continue thanks to the 10 large stashed in the kitchen. The process . . . the struggle is ever going. When I think I've reached a safe and comfortable plateau, I realize that it is at the bottom of a tall and jagged cliff and that the river just crossed with some difficulty is rising to the plain. The stone wall before me is covered with moss, which over time has been dampened by the water now at my knees. To stop is to be swept away by the past. Not to try to fail to reach the future. So I press on.

I wonder if the struggle is the true goal of life. Not to reach the top safely. Not riches. Not happiness derived from comfortable surroundings. But, to struggle. To fight the good fight. And when the struggle is over, or worse, taken away, I seek another struggle. For it is in the struggle that my humanity, my masculine humanity is affirmed. Sometimes, I self-destruct so that I must struggle to rebuild. That is severe and to a large degree unhealthy, but is my way. It was one of the forces in my marriage, my drinking and drug abuse. The rebuilding is not the means but the end. I live for the endeavor. I am whole in struggle.

* * *

Monday's day shift hit the mother lode. There are nineteen deals on the board. Assuming none of them kick, that's a record. The night crew should hit mid-twenties. More friendly chatter and less goading.

"You can take these vacations when ever you want. There are no blackout periods. Take the trips over the Christmas holiday. Bring the kids to Disney. What a great gift for the entire family. No problem with making reservations. Just give us 90 days notice and you're playing with Mickey and Minnie."

"The Silver Sands is a luxury villa-style resort. Every villa has a porch or balcony that opens out to the sea. Your room is filled by the breezes off the ocean. Have you ever seen snow-white beaches before? They're here. You can rent a boat to take a short sail in the lagoon. There is a continental breakfast served in the lobby every day.

Down town is about a ten-minute walk. Steel bands every night on the patio. Just sit and relax to the sounds of the tropics."

"Cancun will be the place for you if you like to party. The Posada Laguna has its own private beach. There are wave runners and sailing skiffs if you really want to have fun. I remember when my fiancée and I were there. We got hooked on wave runners. Bought two when we got home. We're out on the bay or gulf every weekend. Unbelievable. You'll want to have at least one when you get back home. Now . . . ."

"The Big Red Boat is a true luxury liner. Five levels. Huge fore and aft decks for swimming and sunning. Three casinos set the right mood for your stay at the Silver Sands. The Silver Sands has one of the largest casinos on the island. We provide you with a certificate worth $200 dollars in chips to be used at the casino. You can use them at anytime during your stay, but only at the Silver Sands."

"The Posada Laguna is one of the hidden luxuries of Cancun. It's medium size, but with all the amenities of the huge, impersonal places further down on the beach. You'll get personal attention from a professional staff. Your every wish is their command."

"Now we'd like to send this complete pre-approved package out to you in Jackson. The package contains three videos, brochures, your own private Sun Shine Travel ID card, the pre-authorized vouchers and itineraries, $600 worth of coupons and a special 800 number you can call with any questions. This package has a retail value of over $3,000. But, because it is part of our Spring Promotion, and because your name is listed as an award winner, the complete package can be secured for $599. Will you be using Visa or MasterCard to secure the package?

"There is no risk. The package comes to you via registered mail so delivery is safe. The vouchers and itineraries are imprinted with your name, yet they are fully transferable. Take the time to discuss this amazing award with your fiancée. Then decide when and where you will be going first. Take one vacation each of the first three years you're married. Will you be securing this award with your American Express card?"

"We can't send an award package with pre-approved and pre-authorized travel vouchers worth in excess of $2,750 in the mail just for you to look at. This is a special promotion offer. It works like a store coupon. You use the coupon to try the product. And, because it's a good product, you become a loyal customer. After traveling to these three destinations, we know that you will appreciate your vacations and want to use our other travel services in the future. That's why we can offer you a package worth over $2,500 for less than $600. We want to be your travel agent for a long time. Will you be using your Visa card for these vacations?

"You are fully protected by your credit card. Remember that we could not offer you the freedom to use your credit card if your credit card did not approve what we offer and how we do business. You use MasterCard right? Well, MasterCard people come here three times a year. They inspect the vacation resorts and review how we do business. Then, and only then, they give us the right to accept their clients' cards. If they didn't approve of us, we could not take your card. Now, your MasterCard starts with a 5."

"What can you be afraid of? What did you buy your husband for Christmas last year? A set of golf clubs custom made for his height and weight. Hey, I wish my wife were so generous. I got a sport shirt and a floating Styrofoam chair for the pool. But, I'll bet you spent well over $1000 for the custom clubs. And you did that without asking his permission. Right?

Did you charge it on a store account or did you charge your Visa card. Your Discover card, I see. So you took some time to pay off the gift. Well, that's the way to look at these great vacation bargains. For less than $600 you can give your husband the gift of a lifetime. Something you two can share and have memories for ever. If you took the trip next winter, when the snow is at your door, it would already be paid for. No lingering debt. Just a great vacation free and clear. And, for a lot less than the big screen TV. Your Discover card begins with a 6"

"But it's your card, am I right? What I'm hearing, and correct me if I'm wrong, is that your husband won't let you charge anything on your card that he hasn't approved of in advance although you are responsible for the card and the payments. Am I right? Of course, you want to discuss this with your husband. I understand that. I completely endorse that. It's the same with my wife and me. We discuss every major purchase and every major event. But, I trust my wife to make well thought out decisions.

I trust my wife to ask my opinion not my permission when she does something big. Now, I want my children to ask my permission, because I am financially responsible for them. But, my wife has her own job just like you. She makes good money just like you. We jointly run the house and raise the children, but each of us trusts the other enough that we can and do some things on our own. I go fishing on the gulf with my buddies. She goes shopping with her buddies. We each spend our own money. Can you do that? Spend your own money?"

"We could not be in business for fifteen years, if we were dishonest. Tomorrow, I urge you to call the numbers I gave you. You'll be pleased with your decision to secure the vacation package."

"Your MasterCard starts with a 5."

Break is late 'cause the phones are on fire. Never fewer than four in queue. The fish aren't just biting they are inhaling the hook. If any resistance is met, the caller gets dumped and it's off to a bigger fish.

"Jerry, where is the exciting Ms. Grande?"

"How the hell would I know? I work with her just like you. By the way, did you score or should you be diggin' deep to find a twenty?"

"I told you, I think she is a dyke. A carpet muncher. I didn't score. And I never skip on a bet. I'll pay you Friday. Payday. But, Badger has some really strange news. You know your friend who wanted to return the stolen merchandise and money. Well, guess who shows up at the Café Centro Real Saturday morning. The butch, Grande. She tells the man that she has a friend who wants to return the stolen property.

Now follow this cast of characters. You ask me. I ask my friend. My friend meets your friend, Ms. Grande. So it goes without saying that you and Ms. Grande are pals. I mean you ain't fuckin' her cause that's not her style. But you're friends. Now my question is are you the friend of hers who had the stuff all along? Did you and her try masking identities to protect you?"

"Now let me ask you to follow another cast of characters. You know I'm going to Chili's for a night of free food and drink the Saturday night after the murders in out parking lot. Two women show up, lost and looking for directions. They fucked me good. The next time they appear, they are sitting with your friend at the Café Centro Real. Do they work for you or for the man? Do you work for the man? Were you at the café?"

"Hold it. All of this questioning is too much for me. Besides what is really important is that my friend got his goods and money back. He is happy. But, he has informed me that who ever took his merchandise should never even speak of it to anyone."

"Shall we return to the fish?"

"Jerry, you have a call in the office."

Pete looks like shit.

"Hello, this is Jerry Kermasic. How can I help you?"

"Mr. Kermasic, this is Officer Benedetto of the Tampa Police Department. I'm sorry to inform you that your son has been hit by an automobile."

"Where is he?"

"He was brought to the St. Joseph's Hospital Emergency Room."

"How is he?"

"He is resting and receiving the best medical attention."

"Will he be OK?"

"The Doctors are better qualified to answer your questions, sir."

"I'll be there in ten minutes."

My worst fear has become reality. My precious son is in mortal danger. I just saved him from the bad guys and now this happens.

IX

There are some physical similarities, yet huge existential differences between hotels and hospitals. They both are large buildings with many small rooms and a few very large rooms. Each has a courtyard. The layout of each floor is similar . . . like they were created by an architectural cookie cutter. People stay in both for short periods of time. They are both well staffed and the good ones are very expensive. You must pay when you leave. The lobbies are always filled with those coming and going. Big vehicles are parked in the drive circles. When important people arrive, the press and police greet them.

But, and here is the big right turn, the rooms in a hotel are inviting. People want to stay there. Hell, they make reservations. The rooms in a hotel display appropriate amount of utilitarianism embroidered with the optimum in creature comfort. Sometimes to the level of garish indulgence. Rooms in hospitals are strictly utilitarian. Creature comfort is designed to facilitate healing. Functionality rules. People are ordered to go to a hospital or arrive in an emergency without a reservation.

The feeling upon being called to and entering a hospital is diametrically opposed to the feeling about going to and entering a hotel. The former can be described as dread and anxiety, while the latter can be described as happy anticipation. Tonight the dread was ponderous upon my shoulders. Hobbling and hopping precipitously, almost sprinting through the lobby, into the elevator, and down the hall, could not alleviate the pressure. The fear of what I would find at the end of my journey. As I round the last corner in the long hallway, I hear caterwauling reminiscent of the last years of my tortuous marriage. More dread. More pain.

"Where were you? You're David's father. You're responsible for him."

Faster than bullets, her questions were fired at me. More painful than Iodine on a cut, are her comments about my failure to protect my son. More disoriented than a drunk on a loop-de-loop, she sits, stands, and paces. All the while jabbering her attack. There is no logic in this mother's torment. David was staying with her, but the accident is my responsibility. She cannot deal with the reality of her own responsibility, so she sloughs off me all the blame. Any fragment of illogic that she screams loud enough she thinks will deflect the truth. She has worked over the doctor and nurses.

She never mentioned my cane. Maybe she didn't see it through her self-pitied tearful eyes. Maybe it didn't register in her drug-soaked mind. Maybe she was just mind fucking with me. Most of she can spout is a reason why I may be responsible for the terrible event. The office staff surreptitiously leaves the room when I become the target. David looks like a marionette caught in stop action photography. His face is a mask of bandages. A leg and an arm in the air at unnatural angles. Tubes and wires running from his arms and body to bags and monitors in the walls.

"How is he? What happened?"

"How the hell do I know, I'm just his mother. I'm not his big brave father."

"Excuse me. I want to find a doctor. Maybe he'll know."

At that moment the door was filled by a uniformed patrolman.

He must have been six-six and well over 270.

"I'm Officer Benedetto. Are you Mr. Kermasic?"

"Yes, sir, I am. Can you tell me what happened?"

"As far as we've been able to piece together, your son, David, was walking his dog. He came to the Southeast corner of the intersection of Gandy and Himes Boulevards. We're not sure if he attempted to cross, or if he was just waiting at the intersection. But he was struck by an automobile, which subsequently fled the scene. The accident scene is being annualized as we speak. I expect a full and detailed report shortly. I rode in the ambulance with your boy and your wife."

"Ex-wife. My son lives with her. The court felt she was the responsible parent. As you can see they were un-wise in their selection.

Thank you for helping David. I need to talk to a doctor. Need an understanding of the nature and extent of his injuries. Excuse me. I leave you with the boy's mother. Good luck."

"Where the hell are you going now? Deserting your son when he needs you the most. Typical. You never cared for him any way."

I turn on my heels in the doorway, clench my fists by my sides, and stare ferociously at the trembling mass of distorted distress.

"Wrong. I stopped caring for you. You and your drugs. You and your boy friends. You and your *mal de jour*. I couldn't help you, because you had to do it yourself. And so far you've done a marvelous job. I loved David then and I will love David forever. Leaving him in your care was the most difficult thing I have ever done. I must leave this space now to see a Doctor, but I'll be back."

The nurses' station, forty feet away from David's room, is surrounded by a cluster of men and women visually scouring charts, reports, and clipboards.

"Excuse me. My name is Jerry Kermasic. David Kermasic in room 492 is my son. Can anyone give information about his injuries?"

"Sir, I am Doctor Dailey. I am a Pediatric Resident. I can help you. Let's go into the office across the hall and discuss your son. Do you think your wife would like to join us?"

"My ex-wife is near hysteria. If you have been in the boy's room, you know that. Besides, you can tell her alone if you wish. I need to know now."

"As you wish. First, let me assure you that your son's injuries are not life threatening. They are very serious, but not life threatening. He has suffered multiple and compound fractures of his left leg. Fractures both above and below the knee. The trauma pulled open the hip socket on the left. That may have reduced the total damage to his leg. The leg was bent rather than shatter. He has four broken ribs, a broken wrist, and obvious trauma to the left side of his head, and, we suspect minor fracturing of the jaw.

He will have an MRI tomorrow morning to determine if there is any breakage in his skull. Right now, we doubt there is. But I want to be sure. We will not have to operate unless there is something wrong with his internal organs. We doubt there has been internal damage. That's why you see all the tubes and attachments on him. We will closely monitor his vitals, urine and any stools for 24 hours. The broken ribs do not impede his breathing. And his blood pressure and heart rate are within the acceptable ranges for a trauma this extensive. As of now, the prognosis is quite good.

His youth prevented more damage than he suffered. We can repair the bone breaks. He'll have to be in a full leg cast and a chest wrap after he is released. Recovery will take 6 to 9 months. But, he will recover. I can assure you that he will get the best care. We have a number of pediatric specialists on staff and I have taken the liberty to call The Shriners' Hospital for an old friend. I think he is the most accomplished pediatric osteopath in the Southeast. I would like him to look at your son to confirm our initial diagnosis and my plan for the broken bones. Shriners will also help with his rehab.

I'll contact his dentist if you give me his name. He should have a specialist look at the pictures of his jaw. That is not my area of expertise, but the boy's dentist will know someone who can determine the appropriate action. As of now his jaw is held shut with two plastic strips . . . not wired, to prevent any aggravation of the trauma. The hospital will need you or your wife to sign forms and provide your insurance card. Do you have any questions?"

"I probably will have some very insightful questions soon. Just now my head is spinning with what you told me, comprehending the accident, and dealing with the harpy from hell down the hall. I guess I better go to the office. Thanks for the information. I'll check in with you when I return."

Health insurance. Undeniably essential in the western world during the 21st century. More important than clean air and water. A good policy can mean the difference in jobs and futures. The absence of a policy can instigate financial ruin in the event of an accident such as this. My group policy is the last remnant of my last official office job. Carried under the COBRA Act. Cover only my Ex and David. Court ordered. I did not want to spend the money for myself. Macho pig that I am.

Under my present economic conditions, coverage for the two of them costs a relative fortune. Today it is all worth it. Completion of the forms requires that I promise to pay the hospital and the doctors that amount not paid by the health insurance. Sure, and I'll bet they believe in the tooth fairy, too. Back to the room of cacophonous gloom. She seems to be too calm. Maybe before the storm. Then I see her glassy eyes. The meds are working overtime.

"Mr. Kermasic, can I talk to you in the hall?"

Officer Benedetto's whispering does not disturb her trance.

"I just received the crime scene report. It appears that a moving vehicle struck your son without hitting his brakes. There were no skid marks at the scene. The car apparently was making a right turn, ran up the handicapped indents in the curb, and hit David. Then the car drove off the other side of the walkway. The headlamp glass pieces confirm the point of impact. Driving away indicates that the driver was drunk or disoriented in some other way. It was almost dark, and the intersection is very busy and not particularly bright. One of the streetlights had not yet come on. Plus, your son was wearing a dark shirt and slacks. All of these factors contributed to the accident."

"Did anyone see the car?"

"A gentleman, who was pumping gas at the Texaco station claims that he saw a dark sedan speed away in an Easterly direction. A woman standing on other side of the intersection confirms that activity. She saw the car. It was either black or dark blue. Four doors. An expensive car. But, not big like an American car. Maybe European. No one got any license plate information. The car was gone that quickly.

We have sent your son's clothes to our crime lab for a paint analysis. Hopefully, we'll be able to identify the make of vehicle in a day or two from the paint and glass. Then we'll notify the repair shops. That's all I can tell you for now. When I have more information or if I need information from you, I'll call. Here's my card. That's the case number. Please refer to it if you leave a voice mail message for me."

David's mother has nodded off in the chair. Her chin is resting on her chest. Her uppers must have run their course. The room is filled with swooshes, beeps, and pings. Not crying or yelling. No motion from the bed. In the peace that is hospital recuperation, my muscles relax, and I am immersed in the tornado effect of the event. I approach the mass on the bed and whisper to him.

"David, I promise you that I will right this wrong. I will find the person who did this to you and make them pay. Not in money, but in kind. The criminal will suffer as you are suffering now. His pain will exceed his comprehension."

He does no hear me, but I do. And that is the purpose of my pledge. I am in awe of the enormity of the event. Awe rapidly turns to fear. Fear to pity. Pity to self-pity. Was it my fault? No. What could I have done? Nothing. What must I do now? There is nothing I can do here. David's mother will be the sleeping sentry. I'll return in the morning to stand my watch until I must go to work. Hopefully, the-Ex will accept the watch rotation and return for her stand in the mid-afternoon. If not, there will be another verbal donnybrook. I can't afford to miss work. No time equals no pay. It's a simple equation. And, given my bodyguard situation, I am not very liquid right now.

* * *

Tuesday I relieve my-Ex. She is almost pleasant. She is not hysterical. I still cringe in her presence. She agrees to return by three so I can get to work. I promise to call if anything happens. I sit and wait. Newspaper reading is interrupted by nurses checking monitors and bandages. Dr. Dailey, making rounds, assures me that everything is going well. There is nothing I can do, but monitor. Boredom engenders dozing. Suddenly there is motion and a near-human sound from the bed. I'm startled awake. Call the nurses' station with the button at his side. They're in the room in a few minutes. All the while David's eyes do not open. But, he is stirring. Pain and discomfort are creeping to his senses. The stun of the impact is wearing off.

"This is good. His survival instinct is fighting the injuries. The monitors have risen. But, they continue to read acceptable for his condition. Sir, if you talk to him, it will accelerate his return to consciousness. It gives him a target outside his body to spot and on which he can focus. Can you get him to respond to you?"

"David. It's daddy. It's daddy. Can you hear me? Can you open your eyes? It's daddy, David. It's daddy."

Two minutes and his eyes open, but they are blurry. After what seems to be five minutes, he looks directly at me.

"Don't try to talk. Just listen. You were hit by a car while walking Diplomat. I doubt if you remember any of that. But, the important thing is that you are OK. Very sore, but OK. You're at St. Joseph's now. You're getting the best care. Your mother and I are taking turns sitting with you. I'll call her now. I know she'd like to get over here now that you're alert. It's great to see you."

David's mother storms in to his room. It was difficult to reach her. She was sleeping soundly. Or so she said. By the time she arrives, David has been seen by Dailey and two other doctors on the floor. They are pleased. The specialist from the Shriner's Hospital is scheduled to see David tomorrow. My Ex dismisses me to go to work.

* * *

Concentration is important for successful telehuckstering. Got to hammer the objections with the right rebuttals. The ones that seem to answer the questions and promise safety and security but, in reality, don't mean a damned thing. The fish asks about security, I tell them about delivery by registered mail. The fish asks about cancellation, I tell them about how credit cards protect them from making mistakes. Get the card. Get the card. Get the card. That is the mantra. This is still a rich list.

The day shift was on fire. Or at least that's what's on the board. Who knows if it's the truth? By eight forty-five I have two solid. I need a break. Badger follows me outside.

"The bitch is in deep shit."

"Whoa, chill. What's the problem?

"Your friend, the dyke, who returned the stolen merchandise. She cheated my friend. The shit that she delivered was obviously repackaged. The bags were different than the ones my friend uses. So, my friend had the stuff tested. Here's the real kicker, she didn't just step on the merchandise she trampolined it. The crap she returned is nowhere near the quality of the original stuff. She tried to fuck my friend then she disappeared. That leaves you and me with our peckers out. Mostly you. My friend is pissed at both of us and I am pissed at you. I did you a favor and got an introduction. You fucked me over by bringin' in that dyke. She fucked us both over by cheating my friend.

My friend explained to me that it is very bad for his business when someone tries to rob him. It is particularly bad when the thieve gets away with the robbery. Not only is my friend cheated out of his goods and the profit he would earn from the goods, but also the theft encourages other scum to try to steal from my friend. This apparent lack of control not the way he wishes to run his business. So for both our sakes, if you know where the bitch has gone, tell me. I'll tell my friend and he'll get retribution or remuneration for the theft. If not, you will be the object of retribution."

"I have no idea where the woman went. And my being the go-between for you and your friend and her and her friend, who had the stuff, was the full extent of my involvement. I never met her friend. I never met your friend. I'm just the guy who set up a blind date. That's it. So, if you got a problem with your friend. That's your problem. If he wants to get to the woman and her friend, that he can do on his own. I'm out of this whole fucking mess."

Badger's expression is somewhere between rage and panic. I see his jaw jut and his body tense. He's getting his shoes stepped on and he's looking to do the same with me. I must work hard to be calm, yet firm.

"So that's it, eh? An interested party has become a disinterested party. A friend has become a passerby on the street. I'm disappointed in you, Jerry. And, so is my friend. We thought you were smarter than to walk away from those who can help or hurt you. You are part of the deal. And now that your dyke has disappeared, you are the only part that is left. He wants you to reach out and touch the bitch. Tag her so he can spot her. Deal with her. Get both of us off the hook."

"Don't threaten me, Badger. I don't take kindly to threats either from you or your friend. Do you understand?"

"I'm sorry."

"OK. Now we better get back to the room. There are a least four in queue."

"You misunderstood me. I'm sorry."

"I understood your apology for trying to lean on me. 'Nuff said."

As we head through the door, Badger glares at me and whispers, "I'm sorry your kid got hit by a car. I hope he'll be all right."

I am trembling by the time I sit and take the first call. Go through the verbal jousting, while sifting through the wreckage that is my mind.

Officer Willow was right. They are ruthless. Can't call Tony until after the shift. Call from the hospital during my life's job. * * *

"Thanks for returning my call."

"You said it was an emergency."

"You were right. The Lobos are coming after me through my son. Case number RB-34792-00 is being handled by Officer Robert Benedetto. The case involves a hit and run. My son, David, was struck by a car on Monday night. He is presently in Saint Joseph's hospital. I can tell you now the car that struck David was a dark blue Lexus, a new one. He should notify Officer Benedetto. It was driven by one of the Lobos. My guess is that the driver was female.

How do I know this? Badger told me. He didn't actually tell me. He mentioned he was sorry about my son being hit by a car. This fact was not known by the general public, because it has not yet been in the media. Therefore, he knew the fact either before or after the accident. And, since he is a Lobos wannabe, he was told to let me know. He thinks he can earn his bones this way. As a messenger."

"I'll be right over. We need to talk."

* * *

I tell him about stepping on the stuff and the new bags.

"Mr. Kermasic, this puts our case in a whole new light. Now we have an avenue to Lobos. They want to be paid for their coke. We can do that. The downside is that they also want to extract a large measure of punishment for taking their drugs. We have to minimize that risk to get our reward."

"What about my son?"

"What they did to your son, they obviuosly did to send a message to you. Like the two bobbers. I suspect that they think you had the drugs all along and that you used Agent Rivers as a messenger. So they want you. But, they won't kill you before they get the drugs or money. Then they'll come after you. That's your risk. They'll want to make a public spectacle out of the awkward situation. By public, I mean, demonstrate to those in their world how they deal with thieves. They'd probably like to kill Agent Rivers for her involvement in the charade. That's her risk."

"My risk? Her risk? Where's your risk? Where's my protection?"

"Look, Jerry, you got yourself into this bind. You aggravated it severely by trying to trick the Lobos. At the two times when you could have acted like a stand-up guy, you gave in to your selfishness and behaved like a street punk. You stuffed your hand in the cookie jar. And, when you couldn't get your greedy paw out, you came crying to us."

"Easy there Captain Crunch. First, my name is Mr. Kermasic to you. Second, you were all too happy to help me when you thought it would benefit you and your career. I was used by your department. A private citizen coming to the aid of a police department, which couldn't find its ass with all of its hands. We have an arrangement . . . you and me . . . your superiors and me . . . your department and me. I provide. You protect. It's simple. So let's move on. I want to help you get the guys for what they did to my son. You want me to help you get these guys for their drug dealing and general mayhem. I am willing to be the bait, if I have proper protection. Also I want protection for David. Protection so tight that we can't twitch without her moving."

"What do you mean by that?"

"I mean, I want Agent Rivers back in my house until this is resolved. And I would hope it can be resolved in a few days."

"I'll try to contact Agent Rivers."

"Don't try. Do."

"Assuming we can get her, I want something from you."

"And that would be?"

"I want you to be the contact with the Lobos. Obviously, Agent Rivers can't be. It has to be you. I want you to wear a wire so we can get all the information we'll need to wrap up this mess. Our techs have a new micro mic, which cannot be found in a pat down. It's about the size of a straight pin. Can send audible more than four hundred yards. You'll be safe unless Lobos strip you naked and turn you over to the ladies. You don't have a lot of options, so listen carefully."

"I saw one of those mics on the bra of a coed."

The plan takes about an hour to hatch. Tony will have to confirm all of it with his superiors. A wad of flash cash will be required. Others will have to be involved. The more people involved, the greater the chance that something will go wrong. Keep the need to know list very short. I am relieved and relieved of my post.

* * *

Next to my house is a familiar car. She's here. I am elated.

"So, you dicked around with the stuff and I delivered junk. You are a royal screw up. And each time you screw up other people either get hurt or have to come to your rescue."

"Hello. It's nice to see you again, too."

"I thought I could get away with it. Cover my tracks. I thought Officer Willow and his trusted class of clowns would be able to follow the stuff, swoop up the bad guys, and close the case. But, nooooo. They screwed up. They lost the merchandise. They lost the trail to the bad guys. A trail that you and I worked hard and at substantial risk to establish. If they had done what they said could do, we would not be here right now snarling and yapping like two dogs. So don't put all the weight on me. They have to share the weight. Now it's up to me to fix their fuck up. And it's up to you to make sure I stay alive."

"You like this don't you? You like the idea of the farmer as the hero. Rising from the dirt of everyday to right an injustice for a powerless sheriff. You picture yourself as this hero. In your twisted psyche you are an *everyman* driven to heroic deeds by heroic circumstances. In reality you're not the rescuer. You are the cause of the catastrophe. Do you cause the catastrophe just to attempt to solve it? Yes, you do. You need to grow out of that fantasy. That fantasy gets other people hurt. Grow up and take responsibility for your actions, both positive and negative. Do you understand that your boy was nearly killed because of your convoluted thinking? And some grown ups may get killed trying to resolve the situation you created. Do you understand?"

"Yes, I understand. Do you understand that we, you and I, are part of the team that will make everything right? Do you understand that I need to be part of that team?

That I live to be part of that team. Not for the glory, but for the result of the process. I am willing to place my self in harm's way for the jack. I don't have to, you know. I could just as easily demand 24-hour protection for my son until he is able to travel. And then we leave the area. But, where's the jack in that. I'm driven by the jack. I am driven by the racing pulse. The panting. The adrenaline. I need the rush, because it is control and it makes me feel truly alive. Every day I live under someone else's control. I am stifled. I can't do this. I can't do that. I can't go here. I can't go there. But, I dream of the jack that is my control. I understand there are risks in the jack and no risks in the no jack. Between the two, I prefer the jack."

"You're acting crazy. Or as if you're on drugs. And that scares me. Your insanity easily leads to recklessness. And, that recklessness could put me in real danger. You don't live for control. You live for jack . . . the stupid recklessness. You must remain collected at all times to be successful. Control will keep you safe. Jack most often leads to out of control. Out of control will lead to death . . . yours I can deal with . . . mine would piss me off. So, if you can agree to be calm, we can proceed. If not, Officer Willow and I will have to rethink the arrangement. This is your final choice. Either we go on or you get left behind. OK?"

"OK. And, I'm not on drugs. My choice is to be involved. If to be involved, I must be in control of my emotions, I will be in control and I won't let you or Willow know exactly what I am thinking. Enough of this bullshit. I have to go to work now. Badger will press me on the issue. I know I can't react to him. I agree that I must go along with whatever Badger and Lobos want. And, that is most likely big bucks and then my life. It's before the second event that the police step in. I understand all of that. When will I see you again?"

I am crushed. Defeated. Her words have killed my spirit. She is intractable. My rage has been pissed on until it is nothing but ashes.

"Willow and I will come to the hospital tonight after you have relieved your wife. Call Willow when it's safe for us to visit."

* * *

Work is a momentary distraction. Like a gnat in my ear. The list is good and I can succeed despite the lack of attention. I get two. Need a break to get my head on straight. Six in queue. Badger follows me outside.

"I made some phone calls since last night. And I think I have found the mystery lady. Now what?"

"Now, will you tell me where she can be found? I'll tell my friend. He finds her. She gives up the money, plus whatever extra he deems right. Case closed. You and I are back in the sunshine."

"I don't think she'll do that."

"I don't care. What fuckin' choice does either of you have? You tell me, or my friend will deal with you and you will tell him. He will be very angry at you, and his extra will be very great for both you and the bitch. The key is not to piss him off any more than he already is."

"Here's what I suggest. I suggest that you find out how much your friend will take to cancel the debt. I will relay this information to her. She will get together whatever he wants and I will deliver it personally to him wherever he wants. I will be the messenger. No tricks. Just cash for peace."

"What makes you think he will go along with this?"

"Look, you have already shown that your guys can reach out and touch me and my son. Yes, I know Lobos drove the car that struck my son. I know your friend is serious. I am serious about closing this chapter of my life. I'm willing to be the messenger to show that I am acting in good faith. It may take Ms. Grande and few days to get the cash. But, she will do it. She will hold up her end of the deal and I will hold up my end. It is smart for me to make damned sure she holds up her part. Because if she doesn't I will get burned and I will roll on her. She will take the full weight if she fails to deliver. Get back to me tomorrow about how much, where and when."

"I'll need some vig on the deal."

"No fuckin' way from my end. Get your vig from your boss."

"No me, no meet. No meet no exchange. No exchange, great pain. My vig will be 20 percent of whatever my friend wants. I don't have to be a messenger for you, you know. But, if I get my vig, I'll take care of you and the dyke. I'll put in some good words for your two. Live with it or die because of it. Your choice."

"How much do you get from your friend for getting his money? Would he be happy knowing your skimming?"

"I'm not skimming."

"Yeah, right. He tells you 80. You tell me 100. I deliver 100. You deliver 60 and tell your friend that I shorted you. You keep 40 and I die. I know the system, asshole. But, I have a choice. That choice is to make this right with your friend. Not you. So your friend will be accommodated. You'll have to find another way to make money. You can't shake me down. Is that clear? Or shall I simply let it be known that you had the shit and the money all along?"

"Don't threaten me. You will be sorry for your shortsightedness."

Selling is normally insignificant in light of a life or death situation. But, not tonight. The residual rush of my conversation with Badger carries over to my first four calls. I pump through them. I will not take no for an answer. My rebuttals are almost abusive. But, I get two deals. And that's all that matters at my end of the telephone. This is going to be a great week. I'm looking at fifteen minimum. If the list holds, I might get twenty. And it's a B week. Damn I'm good.

X

Another banner day for the day shift. This is the week to catch them all. Badger nods to me. We take a break. Five in queue.

"My friend will take seventy-five large. And, he wants it Thursday noon. Then your slate is clean."

"Seventy-five. You got to be shittin' me. I doubt if anybody could cobble that much money in two days. Give me a break."

"Well chosen words. Because, if you and your butch honey don't come up with the seventy-five, my friend will send his people to visit you. After a few hours of a not very pleasant Q&A session, you will give up the whereabouts of your female friend. Then you will also give up the ability to ever walk normally again. If you think the crutch is an inconvenience, think about no legs at all."

"Where am I supposed to deliver the money?"

"Supposed is not an acceptable word. You will deliver the money to my friend at a place he will designate Thursday at noon. We'll call you at 11:30."

"Noon. Fuck. OK. I'll call you."

"You don't call us. We call you."

"Not possible. All I have is a pager."

"Then we'll page you. And, you call us."

"That's not enough time to pull together that much cash."

"Not my problem is it? By the way how are you doing today? I got one already."

"I got two. I've always been better than you, Badger. And you know it."

His eyes glisten with anger, and his neck muscles tense.

"We'll see who's standing at the end of the race, asshole."

* * *

David looks much better. Truly on the mend. Color coming back to his cheeks. Tubes have been removed. He must remain in the hospital for a few more days. They want to be sure he can move around in a wheel chair once he goes home. They'll train him in how to use the pots and pans. How to wash down. All the things we take for granted. Minor fractures in jaw do not require surgery. Just soft food for six weeks. Urine in the bag is blood-free so are his stools. Doctor Dailey was right. David's youthful flexibility protected him from extreme damage. I told him that my leg injury got worse when I slipped and fell in the parking lot. Have to wear the cast and use the crutch for a while until it all mends. We both got a chuckle out of us . . . a pair of temporary crips.

Enter two officers of the law.

"Mr. Kermasic, Agent Rivers tells me that you are to deliver seventy-five thousand dollars to an unnamed person at a yet-to-be-determined address. Nothing like precision. We can get you the money and it will be discreetly marked. We have the pin mic, which Agent Rivers will secrete on you after you get the call. Plus, we'll wire your car for sound and tracking. The problems in this situation are location and timing.

They will page you at 11:30 for a noon drop they won't be too far away. My guess is the Café again. But, you can't be late. They won't wait. If you're late, they'll accept the idea that you're not coming. If you're not coming, they find you. If the have to look for you, you are in deep shit. So, late is not an option. I think it would be wise if you were to wait for the call downtown rather than at home. They think you live in Tampa and not in the country anyway. So a call from a phone booth should show up on their caller ID as downtown. You and Agent Rivers can be sitting in a car near a booth. Take the page and make the call. Leave Agent Rivers, get in your car, and go to the location."

"Can you get your team to the money drop in time?"

"Not a problem, if you call me immediately upon knowing the address. We'll be on high alert. We'll track you plus we can get to the Café before you arrive. We'll be ready."

"What about me? I just drive through the valley of the shadow of death, find the Prince of Darkness, and pay him his due. Do I get a gun or some form of personal protection?"

"No. Your protection will be all around you when you meet to deliver the money. You'll be safe. I assure you."

"Given your recent record of following the goods, I'm nervous about your ability to keep tabs on me. I'd feel more comfortable with a gun."

Jonny bristles.

"Jesus, you macho fool. They're going to pat you down. If you have a gun, they'll whisk you away, take the money, and kill you flat out. You can't give them any reason to doubt that you are anything but a messenger. Otherwise we will lose the money and our lead. We need you to be passive bait."

"Thanks for your concern about my safety. OK. No gun."

"In fact, you can't even know where the team is. Just understand that they will be there. I'll get the money to Agent Rivers tomorrow morning."

* * *

My two amigos slip off under the blare of the hall lights and I am left alone with my sleeping child. In the shadows of the room, I see my life through him. David as a baby. Happy parents. Birthday parties. A bicycle. Christmas mornings of wanton indulgence. Grade school. His first suit. A dance. Football uniform. A swim party. Vacations at the beach. His grandparents. A big, three-generational birthday party in Pennsylvania.

The images blur. Fade into and out of clarity as I move to another venue. A room of metal tables in fixed spots. I am on one. A cold steel slab. I'm naked under a white rap. Something is on my toe. It tickles. There are people milling around me and the other horizontal mounds on other chrome slabs in this brightly lit world.

The walkers seem to be teams. These moving vertical people wear light green baggy uniforms.

Mine is not a comfortable world. The table is hard, everything is cold, and the repulsion of chemicals fills the air. Odd, my eyes don't sting. The verticals seem to move in deliberate herky-jerky steps. Their actions at the tables are robotic. They bend, pause, mover their hands, become upright, then repeat, repeat, repeat. Some move on to another horizontal. One always stays behind to finish what the others had started. The verticals talk into microphones, which dangle over each table. I don't know how long each stop takes, because I can't see my watch and there is no clock on the wall.

I am talking to them, but no one acknowledges or responds. Does no one hear me? Not the verticals. Not the other horizontals. At the table to my left, a vertical removes the wrap and cuts the horizontal male. No screams. Fluids seep from the cuts and drain through the metal slab. The vertical removes bits, pieces, and parts. Always measuring and commenting. After the cutting, probing, removing of organs, and speaking into the very small mic, two subordinate verticals remove the horizontal from the table and place him on a metal slab that slides into a drawer in a large wall cabinet. I am next. My sheet is removed and I sit up with a start. Sweat and a racing pulse are confirmation of life. An elderly nurse is standing over David's bed. Reading the monitors, laying out his meds, and placing a thermometer in his mouth.

* * *

"Good morning, sir. I see both my boys are doing fine. It must be uncomfortable for you sleep in that chair. What with the cast and all. Sorry, we're not allowed to give you a bed. David is improving remarkably. All signs indicate an early release. He's a strong boy. Now, David, the breakfast cart will be around in a few minutes. Try to eat as much as you can stuff inside. Good food will accelerate your recovery. Dr. Dailey will look in on you before ten."

She scurries out of the room.

"How do you feel?"

"I hurt and I'm uncomfortable. How's the chair as a bed?"

"My minor aches and pains will disappear with a brief walk. Or will that be a hobble. The people here tell me you're making remarkable progress. Home soon."

"Dad? What happened to me?"

"Some asshole jumped the curb while making a turn. You were in the drunk's way. After clobbering you, he sped off. We'll get him. He'll pay for this. I'll see to that. Your mom is excited about your coming home. I think she and I will split your recuperation. She'll take the first two weeks. Then I'll take two weeks. You can live at my house. You'll be alone from 3:30 to 10:30 when I'm at work. But, by the time you're at the house you'll be familiar enough with the equipment and procedures that you can manage for seven hours alone in the house. Besides there is a TV and plenty of incredibly bad junk food. Between the two of us, we'll muddle through somehow. Sound good to you?"

"Getting out of here sounds great."

"What can I get you?"

"Nothing really. I can work the TV and the call buttons. I have a ton of sports magazines. Some swimsuit issues. Have to catch up on my important reading."

I wash up, brush my teeth, and grab breakfast at the cafeteria. Then I just sit. Sometimes doing nothing is doing everything. Can't hover. Can't be a mother hen. This is his process. He must feel some level of control.

* * *

Work is good. The list continues to be hot. Fish just jumpin' in the boat. Get three. The great things about telehuckstering are that there is no homework and no big presentations. Everything is done . . . win or lose . . . within a specific time frame. Just sell, sell, sell. And that time frame is repeated thrice and hour. But, success is dependent on the list, the offer, the script, and my ability to con. To con takes concentration. An event like the attack on David distracts. Muddies focus. I have to rededicate my attention to the moment. It's all part of my process. My control. This week's portion of my process contains a near-overwhelming number of powerful influences: the job, my son, Jonny's return, and my involvement in the police investigation. The complexity and urgency of the elements is the jack. It drives.

* * *

Jonny is waiting for me at home.

"Did you get the money?"

"It's all here in the bag."

"Can I see it? Count it?"

"Sure take a look. But don't touch it. I understand telemarketers have sticky fingers."

"Seventy-five large. I could use this. Where's the exploding powder pack?"

"That's for banks. We use our own way. We insinuated one of the new pin beacons in a stack of bills. That way when they swap out this bag for their bag as a precaution, we won't lose contact with them. We want the snakes to take the money back to their nest. We follow the beacon. Raid and arrest. It's really quite simple."

"Care for a drink? I'm pouring the good stuff."

"No thanks."

"I'm going to be bold. What about me is it that you don't like?"

"Why do you ask that? I don't feel anything positive or negative toward you. You are someone I was assigned to protect. You screwed up, which could be expected from a civilian. Now you're someone I am assigned to make sure doesn't continue to screw up."

"So, I'm just a chair or a lamp to you."

"No you're a human being that is in trouble because of your own stupid, ego-driven actions. And, because of your actions, your son has been injured. It's my job to bring this mess to a close in such a manner that no one else is injured. To do that effectively means that I must still rely on you to perform your tasks. Given your track record, that troubles me."

"Cut me some goddamned slack. I fucked-up. Sure. But, never again. Now will you have drink with me?"

"No."

My feeble attempt at a pass falls flat on its ass. Maybe I wanted it to fail. Sleep is fitful.

* * *

We load into her car at 10:30 and drive to a gas station at North Armenia and East Frontage. My Blue Bolt is waiting nearby, compliments of the police. We wait in silence. Twelve minutes feels like twelve hours. The beep sounds like a factory claxon.

"It's me."

I hop to the pay phone and dial a response.

"OK. Go to 1814 Druid Road in Clearwater. Be here by noon. See you asshole."

"But, that's across the causeway in the middle of noon traffic. I'll never make it on time."

"You're pissing away valuable time by whining. Just be there. We know where your son is."

I hop back to Jonny.

"Jesus, they want me to go across the bridge to Clearwater. And they threatened me with violence to David. I'm pretty sure it was Badger, trying to disguise his voice. What do we do?"

"Just follow their instructions. I'll put the pin mic in the back of your collar. You are connected and protected. Now get going. I've got to take care of business here."

Never thought about the precise amount of time it takes to cross the bridge and head north to Druid. Travel time is normally stated in five to fifteen minute segments of an hour. Today it must be no more that 26 minutes, or I lose. Weaving across the two lanes of the causeway at 85, I arrive with two minutes to spare. The address houses a 7-11, already busy with the construction and trade lunch crowd. Entering, I spot no one I've seen before. No one acknowledges my presence, except to notice my crutch. I leave. The pay phone rings. After eight cries for relief, I answer the black and chrome, dirt encrusted medium.

"Hello."

"Hello, asshole. I'll bet you're glad you made it on time. Now, here are further instructions. Go to the warehouse at 4136 Endicott. Do you know where that is?"

"Drew Park. Right?"

"Bingo, motherfucker. You have twenty minutes from now to be there or be sorry. See you then."

"It can't be done. That's too far. Too much traffic. Can't be done."

"It can be done by some one who wants to protect his child and save his own life. Now, get going."

Panic. How do I let Jonny and Tony know of the second address? By the time they realize I'm going to a new drop, I'll be too far ahead of them. How can they follow me and arrive in time to apprehend the thugs? How can I communicate the change in plans? Simple. They can hear me. I speak to the car's interior . . . like performing a soliloquy on stage. They can follow the car on their scanner.

"Whoever is listening, the bad guys are sending me to 4136 Endicott. A warehouse. They've got David, I think. Or, they are very close to taking him. I've got to get going. No time to chat. Hope you can hear me."

My pager is activated. The alpha message says; *WE WILL BE THERE. DAVID SAFE.* I am a medium for the good guys and bad guys to communicate. It's just that the bad guys don't know it. If I am a medium, my life is at risk. David is safe and I am at risk. This is exciting. Very frightening, but exciting nonetheless.

The traffic is stalled to a creep. A flat tire, tow truck and countless rubber-neckers. Will these motherfuckers move along? Don't they know they're endangering my son? The road's shoulder becomes my personal driveway. Screaming people with middle digits raised are confirmation that they wish they could do what I am doing. Run the two lights at the Tampa side. Leave several cars screeching. Take turns at awkward speeds. The Blue

Bolt performs like a racehorse. I am beginning to sweat. My pulse is pumping. I am jacked. This is the thrill. The speed I thrive on. If it weren't so serious I would be happy.

* * *

Pull into the warehouse parking lot and run to the door marked Office. Taped to the window is an envelope with my appellation in big handwriting. *Asshole.* Rip it open and read the typed note inside.

If you are reading this at any time after twelve-twenty, your son is in deep shit. If you are on time, come to Café Centro Real. You have fifteen minutes. See you at twelve thirty-five. Be late and your son suffers. You're so close. Don't fuck up now.

The throbbing in my leg is a motivator. I scream at no one in particular as I run to my car.

"I'm off to the Café. These bastards are bouncing me from pillar to post. They either know you are with me or they are real sadistic bastards. I have to be at the Cafe by twelve thirty-five. Are you sure David's safe?"

Pager reads; *YES. GO.*

This leg of the race will be hell. Can't take the Interstate. Can't risk the congestion at malfunction junction and the semis that seem to park in all three lanes of the road. Travel on the city streets is an indirect route, and would normally be slower because of the traffic lights. Not for me today. I talk into the air again.

"Here is my route. Kennedy all the way. Downtown. Through the city maze. Out past the docks to Twenty-second Street. Left to the Café parking lot. I'll be speeding and I'm going to need some help at the traffic lights. I suspect I'll have to run a few. Somebody better cover me with the patrol cars. OK?"

Pager reads: *DONE.*

Traffic on West Kennedy looks like a fucking parade. Everybody and their tia Maria are slowly wending their way downtown. That's why the manufacturers put a horn and headlights in their cars. Beeping, blaring, and blinking, the Blue Bolt jerks through and around traffic. Accelerator. Brake. Accelerator. Brake. Accelerator. Brake. Accelerator. Brake. Accelerator. Brake. Accelerator. Brake. This lane. That lane. I shoot through the intersection at Dale Mabry. Drive two cars into the parking lot at Kinkos. I must treat every intersection as if it were an intersection only for other cars. I don't care if the light is green, yellow or red. I'm goin' through. The car is beginning to overheat. Go through 7-11 parking lot to move up in the line of cars and delivery trucks.

Downtown is mired in lunchtime pedestrian traffic. The big building carp are returning for another four hours of mind numbing data jockeying in their cubicles. They eat ice cream and walk at the same time. A real accomplishment. They mass at the corners and ooze into the traffic lanes. The last of the school meanders into the street after the light has turned against them. They become targets of my aggression. Targets to be missed. It is now twelve twenty-eight. Someone has thrown their *Choco-Fudge Cicle* at my car. To give up dessert as a demonstration of rage verifies how close I was to a hit.

I am at the docks. Watch reads twelve thirty-one. Drive like von Tripps on his last day. Won't take out as many as he did, but will take out anyone who gets in my way. Off the street into the unpaved parking area beneath the interstate. Dirt and trash are the foundation of homeless hotel land. Sometimes it's difficult to distinguish the animate from the inanimate trash. Most of the denizens are away from home at this hour. Working the streets for change. Performing menial task for folding money.

No one is disturbed by my incursion. Twenty-second Street is the next light. Suddenly, I feel the car tug to the right and the sickening noise of a flat tire. Fuck it. The thump-crumple-thump is ominous. People on the sidewalk waving to me and yelling that I have a flat. So many friends I never knew I had. Watch reads twelve thirty-four. Two more blocks to the parking lot. Two more traffic lights to run. Suddenly, I'm in the lot behind the Café and out of the car at twelve thirty-five, forty-five. Forsaking my crutch, I gimp toward the front door.

"Hey there sweetie. Care to show an out-of-towner a good time."

"Sorry, but I'm late for very important appointment."

"You're not that late. You're almost on time. Come with us."

I feel hands powerfully grip my upper arms and two bodies press me between them. I glance at the blonde and brunette from the motel. One of them removes the airline bag from my shoulder and the pager from my belt. They plastic smile at me for all the world to see.

"Don't try to struggle or alert anyone. I have an ice pick against your side.

Feel a little prick. Wonderfully apropos don't you think . . . little prick. If you were foolish enough to try to escape, I would be forced to puncture your lung, escort you to an ally, puncture the other lung, and let you die from internal hemorrhaging among the garbage and rats. Die amongst those who know you best. Understand?"

I nod.

"Let's get in our car. We want to go for a ride."

Three of us in lock limp two blocks to a Lexus. As the blonde fumbles with her keys and the bag, the brunette digs her fingers into my bicep. Her grip is like a vise. I will not stray. As she pushes me around the car to the passenger door, she pats me down. Arms, legs, chest, crotch, back. Squeezing and rubbing hard wherever she can. Extra pressure on my left thigh, both above and below the cast. She loves to hurt.

"He's clean."

We bump against the hood.

"Be careful, bitch, the car was just painted."

I am shoved through the passenger door and it is slammed and locked behind me. The blonde tosses the bag into the back seat. The brunette lets me see the gun in her belt. She opens the bag and counts the cash as she transfers to a shopping bag from Burdines. There is nothing subtle about these two. Riding in the car that was the medium for my son's near death gives me a weird feeling. It's almost as if I were in the car as it hit David. Then I get angry. Very angry. Hold that jack. Use it to gain control. Save the rush for another time.

"It's all here."

"Toss his bag and pager."

We slow down at the corner of Cuidad de Castro and Fourteenth. The brunette leaps out of the car and tosses the bag into a wastebasket.

"Where are you taking me?"

"For a ride. Just sit back and relax. It's like you men say about bad sex, relax and enjoy the inevitable."

As we leave downtown and get on to the Interstate, it looks like we're going to the beach or maybe Sarasota.

Take the last exit before the Skyway Bridge and head west two miles passed the Intercoastal Waterway. Then north to the land of the beachfront mansions. 1313 Gulf Boulevard is a palace. White with brilliant yellow accents. Very pleasant to see. Protected from the road by an eight foot wall topped by planters and tiki torches, which I assume are lit by gas. The yellow iron gate swings open. Activated by someone in the house. The circular drive is done in diverse white and yellow brick. The mosaic is a beach scene with a setting sun.

Palms and all manner of tropical plants fill the land from the wall to the house. No windows are clearly visible. No one can look in at the inhabitants. I know why the femme fatals don't care if I know where I am. Fear is becoming panic. The jack is getting too strong. Struggle to maintain control. There is life-preserving safety in control. The wordless trip from the parking space to the large yellow front door is 47 shuffles and about two minutes. Concentration on details is the first step toward control. Like baseball stats before ejaculation.

"Mr. Big Shot, you are here."

"Where is here?"

"Here is where you meet the man from whom you stole the drugs and money. Here is where you meet the man you ripped-off with the bad drugs. Here is where your benefactor will accept your payment of 75 large. Here is where you learn your fate. This is your court of last resort. This is your day of reckoning."

The door opens and we are greeted by a burly man apparently in his thirties. Maybe younger depending on the hardness of his life. He beckons us to follow as the door closes with electronic clicks. I am sealed inside. The house is bright . . . the motif of yellow and white on the outside has many variations inside. The floor is dark stained hardwood. The art on the walls is familiar. I have seen these pieces or their artist's style in magazines. Perhaps, the museum downtown. Obelisks in every corner support traditional and very contemporary sculptures. The central hallway is an art gallery.

Doors off each side lead to rooms essential for living . . . the den, an office, dining room, and library. Glimpses of furniture and décor reveal a high level of sophistication. Most likely that of an expensive decorator. The hall opens up into the living room. Right and left are two half walls facing the twelve-foot sliding glass doors that lead to the expansive deck. The walls, which complete the room, create a space at least 40 feet by 40 feet . . . bigger than a lot of houses. More art, but fewer paintings. The sun fades them. The furniture is light colored wood with dark floral upholstery. Lots of yellow. Couches, big chairs and tables create four separate social groups. We traverse this room and exit through one of the sliding glass doors.

The view of the Gulf is magnificent. Nothing like a private beach. The wall from the front of the house runs down both sides of the property to beyond the shoreline. Looks like about twenty feet beyond low tide. Encapsulated safety.

The deck is as wide, but deeper than the living room. Three yellow and white patio umbrellas over three tables protect two chairs each. The tables are set alike . . . tablecloth, place mats, dinner plates, salad plates, flatware, glasses, ringed napkins, cups, and saucers. Between the settings is a bouquet of Daisies. I am walked to a bench facing a chaise lounge, and visually directed to sit. The burly man walks back into the living room. I wait.

Although the breeze off the Gulf is brisk, the sun is hot on my head and neck.

I stare at nothing and everything. I just sit and wait. Dangling helplessly like the bait before the strike. The surf and the squawking of the gulls fill my ears. This idyllic audio is interrupted by the stomping of feet on wood and the rush of a shower. Splashing of a body in the shower lasts thirty seconds or so. Silence. Then the footsteps as the body wrapped in a yellow and white striped terrycloth robe rises like Poseidon from the beach. Black hair is being pulled back into a ponytail. Oakley glasses have gold rims. Skin tanned and clear. Shoulders broad and chest thick. He, who holds my future does so with well cared for hands. He smiles.

XI

"We finally meet Mr. Kermasic. How pleasant. I hope you are comfortable."

"Nervous, but comfortable so far, Mr.?"

"Monteleone. Humberto Monteleone."

The Big Badger. Unctuous, cleansed and tanned before me. He slides onto the chaise. This is his world and he is in total control. A hand towel is used to pat dry his hair. Leaning back he assumes the role of king on a throne. A Caesar.

"You are here today, because I need you to be here . . . for a while at least. In a few minutes we will be joined by my business associates. These are the same associates who have questioned my ability to manage my business. They have questioned my ability to manage, because you and your childish antics have disrupted my operations. First you stole what was mine. Then, you sold what was mine to that stupid coed. Sir, dealing in the bars of the Combat Zone is the quickest way to get seen. Getting seen is the last step before getting caught. That was stupid of you. But, the bad part was that people thought you worked for me. I am not that stupid. Nor, would I have someone that stupid work for me.

I looked bad, because public exposure is bad. Then, you front another bitch to return my merchandise. And finally, when you return what is mine, it is diluted. Inferior. Not what was stolen. The charade went on for too long. At every stage of this event, you did something to disrupt my business, and hold me up to ridicule. Your actions cannot be tolerated. My business must run smoothly. So, I had to show you that I mean business. The incident with your son is an unfortunate outgrowth of your arrogance and stupidity. I hope he enjoys a full recovery. We need you to pay for lost merchandise and the inconvenience you caused us. The money is only partial payment. The balance will come due shortly."

"Sir, if I may be so bold. Whose idea was the attack on a helpless child? Who drove the car that nearly killed my son David?"

"Jimmy."

With one word, this man had sealed the fate of his relative.

"As a father, I can understand your pain. But, you must understand that my approval of Jimmy's request was strictly business."

"Why is it you guys say it's about the business, when, in fact it is about your egos and testosterone? If it were really about business, you could walk away from a loss. Write it off to a fuck up. Take like a real businessman. Like the President of IBM or General Motors. A lesson learned. Something not to be repeated. But, you can't be objective, because you are not a businessman. You are a criminal.

You always have to hurt somebody . . . avenge an insult, either real or imaginary. And, normally you pick on the weakest or most visible person to hurt. That way your message of physical dominance is seen, understood, and feared by everybody. So, it's not about business, it's about you and your stature in your little dark community."

"We deal in a people business. We provide what people need. We are in the service sector. We are distributors. Distributors of pleasure, safety, and employment. We make nothing. We warehouse nothing. Yet, our endeavors are very labor intensive. We are not on the Internet. Our business is conducted person to person. Like McDonald's, the success of our business is dependent on repeat business from a long-term customer. Like McDonald's, we have many people on our pay roll. Each performing a specific task. They are small-minded people, who must be controlled. We have to control all the details to control the situation. By doing so, we control the outcome of our enterprise.

We have many people, who want to join our organization. Each year we are approached by hundreds of them. They are, generally, poorly educated and of a crude nature. So we have to invest time and money training them. Training them is not easy. It takes maximum control. Just like training dogs. Teaching them the importance of loyalty. Not every dog can be trained to do, as we need done. Many of them are not worth the effort or they get bored or they get foolishly ambitious. So there is a constant culling of personnel. Sometimes this culling is necessarily harsh. It is that way with animals. Watch the Discovery Channel and you'll see that culling the weak is nature's way. To succeed our organization demands loyalty to the organization above the individual . . . even the leader. We cannot tolerate anything less than 100% loyalty.

Loyalty is not always earned but it can be taught by example. Then there are the competitors, who want to take over our organization. Like Burger King or Wendy's. They offer the same service to our customers that we offer to theirs. Or they want to take over our territories. Territories, once expansive, have been reduced to street corners. So, you see, competition is intense. To attract and hold the best people, to cull the weak or the wrong, and to expand our enterprise, we must be aggressive. If we are not aggressive, we will lose good people and profitable businesses. Because of the severity of the marketplace and the personal nature of our businesses, our efforts can appear brutal to those outside our industry. So be it. Our actions are just our normal business practices. And, by the way, our community is not small. Last year, the organization grossed over $115 million. This year we are looking at $160. So we are not small."

The sliding glass door interrupts the *Alice in Wonderland* economics lecture. The short burly man in khakis and a yellow and white striped short sleeved shirt approaches my host. In deference, the intruder waits to be acknowledged.

"What is it, Jose?"

"Your guests have arrived."

"Show them out here. Thank you."

The burly man nods, turns, and heads for the front door.

"We must cut short our conversation, Mr. Kermasic. I have invited my business associates for a working lunch. Before we settle down to work, I will introduce you. So relax for the moment."

The glass door slides open. My host rises to greet the five guests. Four men and a woman. There are faux hugs and cheek kisses distributed evenly. The newcomers are well dressed. Although casual, the clothing has an expensive look. Two men, who appear to be brothers . . . dark wavy hair, prominent cheekbone, high forehead, slanted eyes, and Roman nose . . . are dressed as if their mother were the last one to see them before they left the house. Both are wearing dark green silk slacks. The apparent elder wears a dark orange and green pullover, while the other has on an aqua and light green pullover. Both have black slip on tassel loafers made of Alligator hide and matching Alligator belts.

Then there is a short, thin elder man. Sparse gray hair. Thick wrap-around dark glasses. Like the ones worn by cataract patients. He is dressed all in white. Shirt, slacks, shoes and belt. Very old school Caribbean landowner. There is a couple. He is tall, blonde, terminally handsome, and dressed as if his closet door were the rear entrance to Ralph Lauren's. Very Palm Beach. She is Mediterranean. About five two with a body that would start a war. She almost fits into the floral print sarong. The bulges and cleavage grab everyone's attention. Very calculating. The five are seated at the tables beneath the umbrellas.

"Thank you for coming out to the beach today. It is an honor for me to host this lunch. There are a number of items for discussion. And I hope we can reach agreement about them with short dialog. But, before we commence with the new business, I would you to meet the old business. This is Jerry Kermasic. Mr. Kermasic is the individual, who stole our drugs and our money. He sold our drugs on the street. He made a profit that was not his to make. His activity caught the attention of our friends in the police department. By stealing and selling what was not his, he embarrassed us to our clientele, to our people, and our competitors.

Then when we asked that he make the situation right, Mr. Kermasic had the audacity to return to us cocaine that had been diluted . . . made inferior to that which he had stolen. Today, Mr. Kermasic has partially compensated us for his actions. I wanted you to see him. I wanted you to know that I have taken control of the situation. I wanted you to know that our friends and business competitors will soon realize that I mean business. That I will not tolerate any incursion into our enterprise."

"How has Mr. Kermasic made things right?"

"He has paid us $75 large as a fine for his actions. Now we have the cocaine plus cash. On $120,000, we will make a total $300,000. We will more than double our investment in less than two weeks. All of our enterprise should be that profitable."

"What is to become of Mr. Kermasic now that he has seen us?"

"I will turn him over to my lady friends. They will dispose of him as they see fit. As of this moment, he is nothing more than an encumbrance. Certainly, we cannot let him return to society now that he has been here. But, enough. It's time to scrape this caca off our shoes."

I am dismissed to be dispatched. My host waves his hand and the burly man slides open the door, comes to his boss's side, and whispers in my host's ear.

"Two Japs and a few Mexicans? It's OK"

The burly man clasps my arm and tugs me down the long hallway to the kitchen. There the blonde and brunette, with arms folded, stand in corners awaiting their charge so they can complete their work for the day.

"So, that's it? It's now our turn? This won't take long. We'll be back in about an hour and a half for cocktails. Come along, asshole."

Like a baton I am handed off for the final leg of the race. The thugettes are no less brutish than before. My upper arms are bruised. It is now sinking in. I am being taken to the end. Up to now I have been dazed by the splendor and sophistry of my captors. I failed to realize the process, where we are in it, and my part in it. I behaved like a deer frozen in the headlights of certain destruction. I manifested the beatific countenance of a soon-to-be martyr. I acted like a braggadocio, who thought he could bluff his way out of every predicament. Or who thought he would be rescued from his own failures by the force that always saves him.

Dudley Do Right will not come today. Regardless, I have been a fool. For the first time, sweat appears on my upper lip and in my armpits. A favorable outcome of the situation depends on the communication afforded by an electronic device stuck in the collar of my shirt. And, maybe my wits. Were they able to follow me? Did they hear the conversation with Humberto? How will they rescue me? If I remain calm . . . in control I stand a chance. I must turn the vacillating passion of fear into contemplation and resolve. I must have my own plan for escape.

* * *

"Move it. In the passenger's seat. Take the back. I'll drive."

The blonde is in command. *Nikki Horticulturists* in bold green oriental script with appropriate Japanese symbols designates the enterprise busy removing equipment, flowers and plants from the over-sized step van. Two Japanese and four Hispanics commence their task of assuring the beauty of Casa Diablo. The crunch of shoes on the driveway sounds as if we were in an empty hall. All senses are exaggerated. The leather front seat is too hot. The slam of the doors and the click of the locks are more ominous than the jail door and lock sounds from prison movies. The engine whines to the gate. We exit and turn right as if on a return trip to the city. Not fucking likely.

The distance to the first major intersection is about a mile, but feels like its four feet.

"Where are you taking me?"

"Away. Far away. Far away for ever."

How can I escape the inevitable? When we get to wherever we are to be, I will be dragged from the car. Bound? Not likely. Beaten? Most likely. Shot? No doubt. Dumped in some body of water. For sure. Two against one is too many. If I can kill one, I stand a chance with the other. What weapon? Key ring. Middle finger through the ring and two keys exposed like spikes. Maximum thrust into the neck, just below the chin. Break larynx, rip carotid artery. Simultaneously, I must drive the thumb of my other hand into an eye. I'll have to attack the brunette as she pulls me from the car. Then, grab her gun and fire at the blonde as she locks the driver's side door. Life goes to the swift. Death to the slow afoot. We ease to a stop at the traffic light behind a step van. Suddenly our car is struck from behind.

Simultaneously, two more oversized white step vans with blue *Trilectron* lettering and logos are beside our car. One on the right and one on the left spew forth armed soldiers, whose black garb reads, Tampa PD or DEA or ATF. They are masked. One soldier stands by each of the six windows . . . front, side and rear. Three guns pointed specifically at the driver and three at the passenger in the rear seat.

"Don't reach for your weapons. Put your hands where we can see them. Driver put both your hands on the steering wheel. You in the back seat put your hands on the ceiling. You are both under arrest."

The female voice outside the car is familiar. The time gap between command and response is too long for the commander.

"Freeze. Let me see your hands. Now. You are under arrest. Do it now, goddamn it. Now."

The sighs of resignation are a Hallelujah chorus to my soul.

"Driver, unlock the doors and immediately return your hands to the steering wheel."

The click of the electronic door lock is my signal of freedom. The front passenger door is opened from the outside and I am forcibly extricated by the female in charge. I stand erect as best I can. My two executioner wannabes are yanked from their seats and forced face down on the road for a pat down and cuffing. They are read their rights. I hear words like extortion, conspiracy to traffic, trafficking, prostitution, conspiracy to promote prostitution, kidnapping and conspiracy to commit murder. The two are loaded into the unmarked police car that had struck our car. It hastily speeds into the gathering afternoon. The three *Trilectron* vans disappear and traffic flow returns to the expected in less that ten minutes.

The bug landed on the water. The fish rose to the surface to feed. The eagle dove to the water, clasped the fish in its talons and flew off to feast. All in a matter of seconds. It's as if nothing had happened. The bird, bug, and fish were never there.

* * *

The gardeners have removed their coveralls to reveal DEA, ATF and Tampa PD shirts. They have propped open the main gate to permit entrance by cruisers. The men rush to the front door. Two of them carry a battering ram. The initial pounding on the door is abusive. The command is abrupt and threatening.

"Open up now. This is the police. We have warrants for your arrests. Umberto Monteleone, open this door immediately. If it is not opened by the time we reach the count of five, we will break it down. One . . ."

The burly man instantly summons two others of a similar ilk from the kitchen. Guns drawn they rush to the foyer. Their job is protection of the main entrance. Three others, equally armed, rush to the beach side of the house. Their job is protection of the owner.

Over the walls that separate the castle of crime from the real world pour twelve black clad invaders. Full ski masks and fingerless gloves. All with yellow letters on the back of their jumpsuits. The automatic weapons are trained on the luncheon set.

"Freeze. Stop what you are doing and just relax. Place your hands, palms down, on the table in front of you. You are all under arrest for conspiracy, bribery, drug trafficking, prostitution, conspiracy to commit murder, etc., etc. You can read all the details in the personalized warrants. Mr. Monteleone, please ask your pit bulls to put down their weapons. We have no interest in a firefight.

However, we are prepared to engage in one and will do so as a justifiable event based upon your resistance and the threat of deadly force. So, if you have no interest in becoming a victim of deadly fire, you will tell your men to stand down."

The command is about to be honored as the front door comes crashing in. The three in the front have not heard the command to yield. They are unaware of the force approaching the deck. Their focus has been on protecting the gate. Their backs are to the deck. As the massive door collapses into the foyer, the three begin to fire blindly. Two officers who used the battering ram are hit with 9mm slugs. The officers on the sides of the doorway return the fire into the house. Five firing on three. The three are ventilated by the withering fusillade. Nearly seventy rounds in a narrow area. The devastation is complete. Crumpled bodies ooze blood where they fall. Holes are torn in the walls, the art, and the floor. The noise is deafening. The air is rich with the heady aroma of spent rounds. There are cries from the two officers who manned the battering ram. None from the three, who are in pieces in the hall.

The approaching force and the Monteleone bodyguards in the back of the house are startled by the gunfire. A few rounds coming from the front of the house hit the glass doors that separate the house from the deck. The rearguards think they are being attacked by the men who scaled the walls. In defiance of the command to stand down, they raise their weapons to commence a defensive action against the force approaching the deck. The approaching force outside hears the reports from the front of the house and thinks the bodyguards are firing at them. Then they do. The police adopt a defensive mode.

Scramble and cover. One officer, feeling threatened, returns fire. Then another. Then another. Another.

Three guards and the six diners on the deck are trapped in a torrent of rounds. Their bodies are shredded. The glass doors become memories. Shards bounce on the deck and into the living room. Handles and frames of the doors are dangling remembrances. Torn umbrellas and punctured tables come crashing to the teak floor. Place settings, food, and beverages are strewn over the deck surface. Blood and body parts mingle with the salad and bread. It's all over in thirty seconds. Over two hundred rounds are embedded in torsos and the house. Spent shell casings litter the beach like so many coquinas.

"Cease fire. Cease fire. Jesus Christ. Cease fire."

The explosions reverberate up and down the beach.

"Is anybody hit?"

"Squad Alpha A-OK."

"Squad Beta A-OK."

"Approach with extreme caution and check the bodies. Lance Leader Two to Lance Leader One. Do you copy?"

"Lance Leader Two I copy. Two of my men wounded. Have called for medic. Are your men K?"

"Lance Leader One. All K. Any bad guy survivors?"

"None so far. You?"

"None. Jesus this is going to take a lot of explaining. Hold your weapons, I approach."

Warrants are no longer necessary. The carnage is complete. Body IDs. Round counts and written reports are started before the brass and Crime Scene Investigators arrive. This must be kept out of the news until all the details and a true timeline can be confirmed. Worst-case scenario, this makes the eleven o'clock. Best case, this event is released to the public over coffee and toast at six AM. The police did not control all the details, now the have to scramble to control the perception of what happened.

As we head to Tampa via the back way, the squad car passes the Monteleone house. It is surrounded by squad cars, a SWAT wagon and the two-step vans. The big gate is open and is guarded by two uniforms. I am driven to Café Centro Real and my car. No sign of Jonny or Officer Willow. It's now five PM. After I change the flat tire, I understand the headache of commuter traffic. I am sweating my ass off. Think I'll take a sick day from work. Won't call. Explain the next day. The cell phone in my glove box rings.

"This is Jerry Kermasic."

"Can you come by the station house, we need to talk?"

"I'm still in down town. I can be there in five minutes."

"Good, we'll be at the parking lot door waiting."

Yes they were waiting. Jonny and Tony. Still in black work clothes.

"We wanted to thank you personally for your assistance in closing this case. Without you we would not have been able to move as quickly as we did. We need to give you a heads up as to what happened, what is happening, and what we think will happen. Your two lady friends will be arraigned tomorrow. They will do a lot of hard time. The six people you met before lunch were unfortunately killed in an accidental firefight. I won't go into all the details now. All the necessary details will be in the paper tomorrow. Just understand that the ending of the Loco Lobos is complete . . . for now. And, while this is good, it is only temporary.

The elimination of the six leaders unfortunately creates a power void. What will ensue are intense and violent struggles for dominance. These struggles will be bloody, and they will commence very soon. The lieutenants will attempt to assume the mantels of power. They will form brief alliances to secure their bases. They will break these alliances as they see fit to gain greater power. Those breaks will cause violence. Then there are the threats from outside. Other gangs will rush into the Loco Lobos territories and enterprises like water rushing through a leak. This will generate conflict as the up and coming guards try to protect their own. It's not what we had hoped for, but it's something we had thought would happen eventually. So, we have to round up the lieutenants in the next few days and press our cases against them. Plus, we have to make it very clear to the other gangs that we got the Loco Lobos and we will get them. The net result of all this is that we have a once-in-a-lifetime chance to close down crime in this area and we don't want it to pass us by."

"I will be staying to assist Officer Willow during these next phases. I wanted you to know that my superiors also appreciate your cooperation. And, that until the successful conclusion of the next phase, we are going to keep you and your son under protective surveillance. We'll have someone near you both 24/7. Starting tomorrow."

"So, I'm not out of the woods, but I can go back to my life with an angel on my shoulder. That's some comfort. I guess I'll go back to being a single parent raising a son on the meager income of a telemarketer. We have a house. It even has some extra furniture. What should I do with the bedroom set?"

"Consider it a gift from your uncle."

"Jonny, you're welcome to use it whenever you wish."

"That's kind of you, but I have to go under a different cover."

Her glance at Tony Willow tells me that she has a personal reason to stay in town and she will have a new address for her stay.

There are no smiles from the two law officers. They are all business. I turn, shuffle to my car, and head home. I need to do something before it's too late. I need to keep a promise.

XII

Badger is always the last to leave. But, he never volunteers to help with the shut down. He stays to hustle the last call for the last deal. His car is always parked at the rear of the building. Predictable and ever the loner as his nickname indicates.

"Good evening, asshole."

Badger twists to see the man behind the voice. His hand remains on the key in the door lock.

"Wha? Jerry what are you doing here?"

The *thunk* of the crowbar on the side of his head is my answer. Badger slumps like a sack of wet shit. He seems to sit on the ground after his head slaps the driver side window. The key remains in the lock.

With great urgency, I cover his eyes and mouth with duct tape. Then wrap four layers around his wrists and ankles. I have to drag the blob to my car. Then struggle to get him into the trunk. Fucking cast. He is the cause of my discomfort and my son's injuries, so he must pay. He plops on the filthy carpet. Close the lid with as little noise as possible. Choice: head for home or search his car.

Search. Must be done in less than two minutes. Nothing in the front or under the front seats except for the expected 9mm Glock. Doubt if there is a permit for the piece. Wipe off gun, and put it back. Wipe off the steering wheel, front door handles, and anywhere I touched a surface. Mr. Clean. Back seat reveals nothing. Raise trunk lid. In the wheel well is a familiar airline bag. Part of a utilitarian luggage set? Inside the bag are neatly wrapped bundles of cash. Grab and hop to my car. There'll be time to count the money when the fun is done.

* * *

The light from the half moon is enough for me to wend my way down the drive and into the house without car lights. Dragging the body from the trunk to the back porch with one good leg is an ordeal. But, he bounces well with each tug. Cut the bonds. Sit Badger on a kitchen chair, which is in the middle of the old blanket I took to summer camp many years ago. Crowbar and small Maglite are my tools. Tape legs to legs. Arms to arms. Chest to chair back. The resemblance to a man in an execution chair is complete except for the hood. Rip the tape from Badger's eyes. I want him to see. Remove eyebrows and eyelashes. There goes his chance at the beauty pageant. Tape must stay on his mouth. Silence is golden.

The mixing bowl containing the liquid is on the table. The combination of household ammonia and bleach creates a crude form of muriatic acid. Muriatic acid is great for removing scum from the tile in bathrooms and air pollution from marble. It is also very effective rejuvenator of the unconscious. The fumes gravely irritate the cilia in the lungs of those who inhale. Respiratory discomfort is intense. Breathing becomes labored, phlegm and mucus are coughed out, and wheezing for ten minutes after inhalation is common. Prolonged use results in permanent damage to the lungs. That would be the least of Badger's problems.

His form is lifeless. I place my ear over his nose. He is inhaling and exhaling. Very shallow. Time for the magic potion. I dip a small dust rag into the liquid. Two waves of the wet rag beneath his nose cause him to stir ever so slightly. His head bobs and weaves almost gracefully. Then I shove the rag against his nostrils with my left hand and slap his chest with my right. Priming the pump. The inhalation is deep. The coughing and sneezing are instantaneous.

The tape over his mouth prevents Badger from discharging that which his lungs wish to expel. He can scream, just not be heard. Tape and distance from other ears are a wonderful combination. Coughing beneath the tape causes the semi-gelatinous fluid to pump from his nose. His eyes are open and enlarged by fear. Tears pour down his cheeks. The headache he received in the parking lot is a minor concern. Breathing is paramount.

"Just relax asshole. The more you struggle the less you'll be able to breathe. If you relax and don't attempt to scream, the coughing will subside and almost normal breathing will resume. Do you understand?"

He nods over his coughs.

"We're going to take a break while I explain what this is all about. First let me assure you this is not about business. This is strictly personal. Well, there is the matter of the bag from your car trunk. In that respect it is business. I will keep the contents as payment for the bet you lost, compensation for insults, and for my son's medical bills and rehabilitation. That's where it's personal. You see, if you had just left him alone, you wouldn't be here and I wouldn't take your money. Funny how that worked out. I know you drove the car that struck and nearly killed David.

How do I know, you ask? Some thug named Humberto Monteleone told me that he let you do it. He said you wanted to do it to teach me a lesson. Tonight you are going to learn many things. I will be the teacher and you will be the student. You will receive many lessons. A lesson in pain. A lesson in fear. A lesson in responsibility. And, the ultimate lesson . . . the lesson of life. This thug, Humberto, is dead now. I didn't kill him. The police did. In fact they killed all the leaders of your unholy business venture. With their deaths, you could have moved to the top, but it just wasn't meant to be. Do you understand?"

Badger's eyes are now squinting at me in anger.

"I'm going to fix a drink. Sorry I can't offer you one. But, as you can imagine, removal of the tape from your mouth is too big a risk. I bought a special bottle of Scot's Whiskey for this occasion. Nearly $85 for the Balvenie, but it's worth it. By the way I spent some of the money I stole from your chicken-shit gang to buy the nectar of the clan. Did you ever spend that much money for good whiskey? Probably not. Excuse me while get the bottle and some water."

While in the kitchen I hear his struggling. The chair legs produce a muffled scrape through the blanket on the concrete floor. Can't let him get too far. Stroll back with two bottles and a simple Waccamaw tumbler.

"Well, you have energy. That's good. Fear fosters fight or flight. Which is it for you? It matters not. Soon I will decide. So just be still for a second. Let me move the table a little farther away, so that it doesn't accidentally tip over spilling your resuscitation potion or my adult beverage. That's better. Would you like to know exactly what is going to happen? Good, I'll tell you. I'm going to hurt you the way you hurt my son. Then I'm going to free you to save yourself. If you can make it to freedom, good for you. If you can't, good for me. I think that's fair, don't you? No. Well, tough shit, you don't get a vote. This is not a democracy. This porch and the house of which it is part are my domain. I am king. My word is law. I am in total control. Now on to the activity of the night. Pain. Excruciating, mind warping pain. First your leg."

His wiggling and bouncing are to no avail. His eyes alternate between pleas for mercy and daggers of anger. I go to the corner of the blanket. There is a True Value pry bar. I grab one end and raise it to Badger's eyes.

"See this. It's not the finest forged steel. It's Japanese. It will serve my purpose. Breakage. Now let's see. The doctor told me that David suffered two breaks in his left leg. One below the knee and one above it. I think the tibia is the one below the knee and the femur is above the knee. I'll start with the tibia."

The *thunk* is a prelude to the sound of cracking bone. Badger's muffled scream is followed by silence as he passes out. I go to the table and refresh my drink. The Scots have a way of blending, water, dirt, and flowers, then storing this mixture in wooden barrels that have been burned on the inside. The storage lasts fifteen to thirty-five years. In the case of this particular nectar, the storage is in two different casks. One, which held burnt peat and one, which previously aged sherry. It is these latter casks that the nectar is finished. When the barrels are opened, the liquid has been magically transformed into ambrosia. Balvenie has a smooth, almost sweet finish with little or no snap of alcohol.

My charge is not going anywhere. So, I can take a break. Oops, bad choice of words. The chirping of crickets, tree frogs, and other assorted critters provides symphonic background to my efforts. Limp walk to the car and retrieve the third bag of the set. Back in the kitchen, I unzip the bag and dump its contents on the table. Out of the maw plop eight, nine, ten packs of bills. Fifties and hundreds. Twenty-two thousand dollars . . . my treasure trove. In ancient days, the executioner kept all the booty from the executed. So be it today. Back to my motionless subject. Once again I place my ear at his slobbering nose. Inhale. Exhale. Inhale. Shallow, but activity nonetheless. He lives.

Phase two. The wet rag is placed over Badger's nose, again. His heads snaps back. Coughing and twitching commences. Globs of fluid pulse from his nose. Eyes open with nothing but fear in them. No anger. He knows I am in control. This is real jack.

"Hello, sleepy head. Yes, you're alive. Yes, the pain is real. Yes, I administered the pain. Yes, there will be more. While you catch your breath, I'd like you to know that I find it interesting that the bag in the trunk of the car is a match for the bags from the trunk of the car I stumbled upon that fateful night. My guess is that the drug deal in the parking lot was your idea. The drugs and the money were your responsibility. When your deal went bad, it was your idea to kill the two, who fled. You needed to cover your tracks. That's how you knew the message behind their murders. Am I correct? Good. You, Jimmy, are a bully. Blaming others for your failures and harming children. So, in the tried and true old-fashioned way, the bully will be treated as he treated others. Do you understand? Good. Now, if memory serves me, the next break in David's leg is the femur. So . . . are you ready?"

Badger squirms. His whining is muffled, but heartfelt. He tries to move the chair away from me in the dim light of night. A firm hand on his shoulder stops all struggles. I raise the crowbar. With all my righteous indignation, I slam the black metal wand of pain administration onto his left thigh. The chair seat cracks under the force of the blow. Badger's quiet howl is brief as his head slumps still on his chest. I examine my handiwork. The blow to the tibia has produced blood at the point of impact. The tear in his trouser revels what appears to be a shard of bone protruding from the wound. Blood is barely noticeable at the thigh wound. The dark patches are beginning to drip on to the blanket. The only way to be sure the femur is broken is to grab his knee and move it left to right. Doing so, I notice the upper part of the thigh does not appear to be firmly connected to the part directly above the knee. This movement increases the blood throb from the strike point. A successful phase two. Time for a break in the action. Oops, there's that word again.

"Stage three will be much less painful, Badger. I promise you that. Oh, that's right you can't hear me. Let me remedy that."

The filthy rag of revival is dipped and held under his nose until his head snaps back. The coughing begins. Eyes are not opened. Blood appears at his nostrils. This means that the acid fumes are burning his lungs. No doubt his throat is also bleeding. Blood from various parts of his body is a good thing. Coughing and saliva cause the duct tape over his mouth to puff out then in as he tries to catch a breath. But, each intake is loaded with acid that causes the coughing, which aggravates the phlegm and the mucus. The gooey mixture is forced into his mouth and nose. Some of it escapes the nose. Most of it is swallowed, only to be coughed back into the nose and mouth. The cycle continues until the spasms cease. Breathing is labored, but possible. Slowly his eyes open. The flashlight into them causes them to flicker.

"You're still alive. Would you like some more wake-up perfume? No? OK. Listen to me, Badger. We only have two more phases to go through. Then you'll be freed. Understand? Good. Let us go forward, as they say."

Before he has a chance to consider the situation, the pry bar crashes into his left rib cage. The blow is not as severe as those to his leg. It is meant only to break, not crush. Blood and internal fluids spew from his nose. He collapses. Time for me to take a pee and refill my glass.

"Stage four. The final stage before you're freed. Stage four is the wrist. Oh, once again I have erred. You can't hear me from your deep slumber. Let me help you awaken."

The rag is dipped, but not wrung out. I slam up Badger's nose and hold it for at least twenty seconds. His gulping is audible. His body struggles to reject the fumes and liquid that cut into his breathing apparatus. More blood than phlegm or mucus comes to his nose. His head is snapping with each inhale and each internal repulsion. Eyes now plead for relief.

"Glad to see you, too, asshole. One more phase. Then you're out of here. OK? Good."

The crush of the crow bar shatters his wrist and the arm of the chair. Back to nightmare land for Jimmy. This gives me time to cut loose the tape that binds, wrap him in the blanket, hoist him up to my shoulder, and schlep the sack of shit to the wheelbarrow. Place the remains of the chair on top of Badger, who is resting uncomfortably in the wheelbarrow. Place the revival rag and some fluid in a baggie, which is tucked into my shirt pocket. Begin the trip to the lake. Pushing a body-laden wheelbarrow over sandy dirt and scrub grass to the lake with only one good leg takes forty-five minutes and exhausts me. There is Bob Potter's fishing boat. I dump the contents of the wheelbarrow into the boat. The noise reverberates across the Baton Lac. I push the boat and its cargo into the water.

* * *

Like Charon, I row my passenger toward the other side . . . toward the stand of mangroves. I slump over from fatigue and rowing. In slow and near perfect rhythm I pull the double oars. Very slowly the vessel glides over the still water. The moonlight bounces like shards with every oar stroke. The dip and pull process creates swirls of alternating dark and light. One to the right and one to the left. Tight circles widen and diffuse. This is a new pattern on the water. This disturbance to the tranquil water emanates from the back of the flatbed creating a symmetrical V. There is no reason to hurry or panic. I am in control. My final jack of the night.

Well beyond the middle is the place to stop. Boating the oars, I crawl to the fore half of the flat bed . . . to the blanketed traveler and chair. Carefully I lower the chair overboard. After a muted splash, it gradually sinks and is absorbed into its new environment. It will remain in limbo between silty bottom and tranquil surface until it is completely water logged. Air bubbles rise after the object is no longer visible. The bubbles sparkle in the moonlight. I grab the baggie, remove the rag and push it up Badger's nose. It takes some time for his eyes to open. They are glazed. No anger. No fear. Not yet. He starts to wiggle. Then buck. The boat rocks. I stay on hands and knees so as not to tip the craft. The boat rocking signals the dragons.

Badger is beckoning his executioners. It's time for me to make sure they can meet the condemned man. I splash the oars. The water begins to roil and froth on each side of the ferry. The dragons will think there is something special out here. They would be right. Enough invitation. I cut the tape and release the criminal. He has been freed as I promised. I reach under Badger's battered body and start the expulsion from the boat. Very difficult given my bum leg, his near dead weight, and his position on the bottom of the boat. With great effort, I raise his mass to port and roll him into the water. The boat damned near tips. It rocks back and forth taking on some water. Badger's splash-'n-plop confirms he is away.

After the initial submersion, his natural buoyancy will bring him to the top. Then his struggle to survive will begin in earnest. First he'll remove the tape so he can breathe, then he'll try to swim. Labored breathing, his disability, and complete disorientation will probably drive him in a circle. But there will be much activity in the water. Bait trying to escape. From the far shore will come the assassins. They will navigate their territory with ease and stealth. Approaching Badger, the dragons will accelerate to full speed. He will sense their presence about three seconds before they hit. Long enough for unmitigated panic to grip him like a vise. Freeze his activities so that he won't be a moving target.

I slowly row away from the drop spot to the safety of my shoreline. The rhythm of the dip, pull, and return. The small eddies swirl out from port and starboard. Most of the lake's surface is flat. This is quite peaceful. Almost idyllic. About a hundred yards from the pier, my reverie is interrupted by Badger's thrashing and the plaintive cries for help. The cries become epithets directed toward me. He doesn't know it now, but this is his death rattle. His clamoring caroms off the surface and reverberates to the shore. Then there is an explosion in the water. The two have arrived. The water churns. Arms, heads, and tails flop. The smacks create white water . . . a circle about twenty feet in diameter. The cries intensify and are stilled. The water is still. Only the froth marks the spot. I return to my return. The subtle splashes of rowing are foreground noise. The chirping of night critters is the background. The moon beacons my return home. Soon I will rest after a job well done.

Jimmy, you harmed my child. You committed the ultimate sin from which there is no redemption. I promised David that the person who harmed him would suffer painful retribution. Promise kept.

XIII

"Thank you for calling Sun Shine Travel, this is Travel Coordinator Denton. How may I help you?"

"I was calling to see about this vacation I won."

"Ma'am, on the certificate . . . do you have the certificate in front of you? On the certificate at the upper left-hand corner, you'll see a certificate number. It starts with two letters and has five numbers. Do you see it? Will you read it to me?"

"If I give you the certificate number, I haven't bought anything have I?"

"No, ma'am. But, I need the number to activate your award file and to verify that we sent the proper certificate to the correct individual."

"OK. The number is RB36487."

"Thank you. Now if you can hold for a moment, I have to go to the main frame and enter your certificate number. This will lock it out. That means no one else will have access or can take your award. Can you hold?"

"Sure, but I ain't buyin' nothin'."

"Ma'am, I just want to make sure you have all the details of the award and that no one else can get your award. I'll be back in a moment. Thanks for holding."

Time to get a cup of coffee while the fish circles the bait. The on-hold message will soften her up. Testimonials from happy vacationers. Phony background sounds of surf, island music, and children. Voices are those of the telemarketers. Paid $50 each.

"Thanks for holding. Sorry it took so long, but there were a few other people waiting to claim your award. I had to verify the exact time of your call. You beat them out by ten seconds. It's officially your award. Now, how can I help you?"

"I need to know the details of this prize."

"That makes sense. The certificate can only give you a brief outline of the award. It's only a sheet of paper, right?"

"That's right."

"Before I start, let me remind you that you called on our special Award 800 number. And, therefore, this call is not costing you a penny. Second, I want to give you all the details of the Award. So, please feel free to ask any question anytime during my explanation of the details. Don't' be bashful. Interrupt if there is something I am not making clear to you. OK?"

"OK."

"First, a few details. Let me verify your name and address. Are you Ms. Jane Salmon?"

"Yes."

"And, Ms. Salmon, do you reside at 20 Race Avenue, Lancaster, Pennsylvania, Zip Code 17602."

"Yes, all that's correct."

"Great. I would like to suggest, if you haven't done so already, make sure you have a pen and pad of paper in front of you to take down any notes on the details I'm about to give you. OK."

"Way ahead of you."

No you're not.